PRAISE FOR **LOVE AT LAST SIGHT**

"Love at Last Sight spills with witty, intelligent stories that sneakily uncover the secret rococo in the everyday. Bowering's gift makes her version of the familiar frightening but still desirable, unexpected and funny. Every story in this collection is a jewel."

—**Suzette Mayr**, author of *Monoceros* and *Venous Hum*

"This stellar debut collection of stories—mercurial, polished, philosophical, funny—is a series of histoires d'amour set in the bars and streets of urban Edmonton, written with multiple ironic voices. Thea Bowering has a knack for locating the instabilities of the literary present in these gifted, lively tales about memory and perception, love and conduct."

—**Sharon Thesen**, author of *The Good Bacteria* and *A Pair of Scissors*

"Thea Bowering's comprehension and skill with the short story is extremely enticing. Love at Last Sight is a wonderful display of a finely balanced poetic intelligence applied to this narrative form. The stories are full of books and authors, mythological, and personal echoes; Roland Barthes, Robert Kroetsch, her own upbringing in the midst of an intense literary household, frame a vibrant pastiche of biofiction. Her craft with the paragraph, that hard nut to crack in writing prose, is one of the best I've seen in Canadian fiction. Bowering's project here is to use the story as an innovative witness to the range and magnetism of her own moment."

—**Fred Wah**, author of *Diamond Grill* and Canadian Parliamentary Poet Laureate

LOVE
AT LAST
STORIES
SIGHT

Thea Bowering

Oct 4/13

NeWest Press

For Jaime,
thanks for
coming, I
hope you enjoy
these ♥
Thea

— — —

Library and Archives Canada Cataloguing in Publication

Bowering, Thea, 1971-
          Love at last sight / Thea Bowering

Short Stories
Also issued in electronic format.
ISBN 978-1-927063-34-7
          1. Flâneurs--Fiction. I. Title.

PS8603.09745L69 2013   C813'.6   C2013-901533-7

— — —

Editor For the Board: Jenna Butler
Cover & Interior Design: Greg Vickers
Author Photo: Laughing Dog Photography

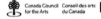

NeWest Press acknowledges the financial support of the Alberta Multimedia Development Fund and the Edmonton Arts Council for our publishing program. We further acknowledge the financial support of the Government of Canada through the Canada Book Fund (CBF) for our publishing activities. We acknowledge the support of the Canada Council for the Arts which last year invested $24.3 million in writing and publishing throughout Canada.

 201, 8540–109 Street
Edmonton, Alberta I T6G 1E6
780.432.9427
www.newestpress.com

No bison were harmed in the making of this book.

We are committed to protecting the environment and to the responsible use of natural resources. This book was printed on 100% post-consumer recycled paper.

1 2 3 4 5 14 13 I Printed and bound in Canada

This book is dedicated to my father,

GB–

The delight of the urban poet is love — not at first sight, but at last sight. It is an eternal farewell, which coincides in the poem with the moment of enchantment.

—WALTER BENJAMIN

"On Some Motifs in Baudelaire"

TABLE OF CONTENTS

FINE ARMOUR

A chantar m'er de so qu'eu no volria

(It will be mine to sing of that which I would not desire)

— La Comtessa de Dia

We are no longer quite ourselves.
As we step out of the house on a fine evening...
[We] become part of that vast republican army of anonymous trampers,
whose society is so agreeable after the solitude of one's own room.

— Virginia Woolf, "Street Haunting: A London Adventure"

There's nothing soft about me. If you look around my room, it looks hard, like a man. A young man's room—monochromatic and all angles. It's misleading, therefore, that my roommate's taken to greeting me with "M'Lady" when he walks in the door. A joke. There's nothing M'Lady about me, but my roommate is studying the troubadours; they're the final requirement of his English degree. The truth is, my roommate is far more M'Lady than I am, or rather, he's like all the boys I know, who are like these men, crusaders-turned-poets, who all looked like women. Well, not women, but the thing called feminine. Not Fem. Feminine. And I hate this word; who uses it? It's right up there with saying "panties" instead of "underwear." It makes you think of things like scented tampons: pink plastic bullets sprinkled with "Meadow Rain" or "Eternal Spring." And even the women I think of as refined find this innovation fairly horrifying. I mean, who wants to bleed all over Eternal Spring? I know only one woman who has used these fragranced plugs: my friend Skip's grandmother. He says she bought everything in bulk her whole life, so for years after menopause she used tampons in her hair as curlers.

My roommate lets his hair grow long, into yellow ringlets, and collects things like candlestick holders and masks. He wears a light fabric vest with no shirt under it. I should mention that this is the early '90s, and that my roommate is an aspiring musician. If you recall, in the alternative music videos of the early '90s all the singers look like pirates trying to look like medieval poets. The only ones wearing skinny jeans are rockers and skaters. No one is marketing "your boyfriend's jeans" for girlfriends yet. The boys I sleep with wear my clothes; I wear theirs. It's that simple. I like sleeping with people my own shape and size. Before they leave in the morning they borrow my hairclips and elastics, my necklaces and shoulder bags. And they can push more silver hoops through their ears than I can. I'm still fairly young and think they're sensitive.

If there's any difference between us, it's not in our couture; it's in the way we live in rooms. The boys still do all the rewiring around the place, but while they're out playing their guitars to girls somewhere, I have stopped midway through the week's worth of dishes to become suddenly despondent by the lack of a translucent blue vase on the mantel, a blank space on the wall where a sparkly mirror should be. I have moved crappy furniture around and around apartments with women roommates all my roommate-ing life. We stand, eyes darting, fingers to our mouths, hoping thriftstore-shabby will pass for '70s SoHo.

So, it's the early '90s, and gender has just begun to get in trouble, and this "M'Lady" thing started about a week before I started telling you about it. "What are you studying?" I yell into the living room, from my bedroom, where I am arranging an alley-find into mid-century Danish modern. "Fine Armour!" the roommate yells back. I stop, and picture knightly medieval men prancing in breastplates etched with delicate flowers, like the ones on my grandmother's tea service. Maybe I heard right. I reach for a lexicon (there's no internet yet); it looks like "Fine armour" is mentioned a lot in *The Iliad*. When Achilles goes off to kill Hector, and has to fight his way through floodwaters, he witnesses the "goodly armour" of youths drifting about, alongside their corpses. Scamander can't handle Achilles' godlike arrogance, so he raises the floodwaters and yells that neither his good looks, nor his strength, nor his "fine armour" will save him now! Still, what does this have to do with the troubadours? I wonder. "What?" I yell again to the roommate. *"Fin Amour!"* he yells back. "Oh!"

Apparently, there was this brief moment in European history when Man's greatest desire was to become a hot, untouchable Lady. My roommate shows me a book of some paintings from the 12th century. A girly poet lounges on a green hillside, heart-shaped head in hand. Next to him his manuscript folds over itself, suggestively, while exotic birds fly through it. On the facing page, a Lover and his Lady sit in a bedchamber. White paper falls from the ceiling, to divide them. A poem on a hymen-esque scroll is as virtuous as a knight's sword. Both are smiling coyly. They look just like each other. My roommate says it's because the knight-poet feels he is, at last, as fine as his Lady. Back from spearing Turks and horny as hell, he knows it's time to wash his hair and clean up his act. He's desperate to get behind his Lady's courtly walls because, my roommate says, he wants to be her as much as do her: become a gentleman, learn some restraint, get some morality, write better poems. However, once he's set up shop, this Christian gentleman will settle into a good night's read of Dante, who will offer up his desirable, but immortal (read: prudish), Beatrice. With that, this brief moment of the powerful, though carnal (read: likes sex), Lady-of-ambiguous-gender will become, *pfft*, kaput.

I get busy moving my heavy, squarish, seemingly masculine room around. I sleep on my great-grandfather's bed; my desk is where my father wrote his first novel. My father mentioned these bits of heritage with pride, which was surprising since my dad's not much into heirlooms in general; though I found out the dusty felt thing in his dresser is a skullcap that belonged to his father. My grandfather wasn't Jewish; he wore it at night to keep his hair down. I guess he awoke with hair as ridiculous as my dad's. Usually, my father is trying to get away from all the stuff in the house. It's as though the stuff in the house and the stuff in his head are locked in a lifelong battle. I read somewhere that you don't really know a picture or an object until you've dusted it every day. It's like typing a book instead of just reading it. I may have gotten this from *The Autobiography of Alice B. Toklas*. At any rate, judging from the dust piling up like snow around my dad, typing away in his study, he never gave the world of things a chance.

Just as surprising as the above-mentioned bequeathing was the time I heard my dad call himself religious. I didn't realize this had to do with the fact that my dad was a poet, not a churchgoer. So I mistakenly decided to take up Sunday School for a while. This was easy because the church was across the street from our house, and because the neighbour's kid went. The neighbour-kid's parents took me because Sunday School came on right when Sunday Major League Baseball did, which my father attended religiously every weekend. I started to get suspicious, though, when all we did was colour in pictures of Jesus. There was a crayon the colour of a dying goldfish, labeled "skin colour," and a baby-poop brown one for Jesus's beard.

One Sunday, I opened my colouring book to find a full-page spread of God. His long hair swirled into the clouds, and he seemed to be in his pajamas just like my dad always was, most days when he was working at home. God pointed his forbidding finger down at something outside of the bounds of the colouring book. It was like how my dad pointed at the countries and capitals he wanted me to memorize, from the map he stuck to my bedroom wall, or how he pointed at one of our eight multiplying cats, yelling "Get out!" We used to have two cats. Then, after a play in the downtown East Side, my parents found themselves being followed by a beautiful, meowing stray with long red hair and big blue eyes. My dad named the cat Menzies, after the flaming red-haired Scot, Dr. Menzies, who was the right-hand man of Captain James Cook, and, my dad implied in his historical novel, a bit of a poofter. In nature, there isn't supposed to be such a thing as a red-haired, long-haired female cat. But Menzies was a miracle of nature, and, we found out, more like a Romantic Heroine than a Dr. She turned out to be pregnant, and before you knew it, word got out and people just started throwing their cats over our fence. I deliberated for a second about God. Yellow? White, maybe? I had neither colour. Dying goldfish pink? Baby-poop brown? I wrapped up my small collection of crayons in an elastic band and quit Sunday School.

As I push around my boxy heirlooms, I picture father after father rolling over to sleep, with their heavy white heads, where I roll over now. For me, the bed's history is not in my hands, but deep in its own thick, worn brass. Still, at times, I have wanted to apologize to my dad for not passing down the history of the Bowering men. I feel his descendentless woe as he reads out the RBIs of ballplayers over the newspaper at the breakfast table: a comic routine, since he knows neither my mother nor I are actually listening. I feel it when I recall how he coached my elementary school's all-girl baseball team. From the sidelines, he yelled at my girlfriends for chewing on their mitts during the bottom of the ninth. My dad would like to have told a son about the desk and bed. Maybe it doesn't matter. Maybe I am, partly, a son. Or his own ideal self. In my father's poems, I don't get much older than ten, and as with those early travelling poets, or Dante, sometimes I think it's his own light his eyes see when he looks at me—as though I'm the thing he's using to get the poem where it's going to. My roommate tells me there were some female troubadours, and they talked about the same problem. They got tired of being remote Ladies, ignored in real life: *I wonder where your heart is, for its house and hearth are hid, and you won't tell.*

Because everything's weighty, I throw colourful fabrics about. I figure this is what women do, drape things for a cottagey, French-like feel. I enjoy layers, not petticoat layers, but the lovely, starchy layers of hotel sheet confinement. I have a friend whose father disappeared when she was little. Every night, she would cram dozens of small stuffed animals between the sides of her body and the bed until she had a firm outline of herself, and could go to sleep. Me, I arrange body parts around my room: an alligator-head bookend from Louisiana sits on the nightstand; the torso of an old wood puppet lies on a window frame. Figurines and small dolls repel me, though—I think because of our visits to Aunt Ball's growing up.

In Aunt Ball's small town, in her small bathroom, when you sit on the toilet, you are eye to glassy eye with a life-size, hollow, pink crocheted poodle. With his crocheted curls, he is the keeper of the extra rolls of toilet paper. At Aunt Ball's, anything you might consider indecent is hidden under a crocheted outfit: the legs of chairs, the Kleenex box. When we visit, I am always put in Pam's old room. It is the kind of room I will spend a lifetime trying to stay out of. Filthy-white, knitted creatures slump on top of each other at the head of the bed. They gaze at the seldom-disturbed crocheted bedspread. A crazed light pools deep in their green plastic eyes, as though they miss the girl who tossed hotly, pressed them to the wall until they became flat and matted on one side.

On the wall are two cameos of two girls with upturned noses and long hair in bows, black against an apricot background. They face each other, but are staggered, so not looking at one another. "They were done of Pam and her sister when we went to Disneyland, but I can't tell them apart, can you?" Aunt Ball asks me. I could not. The only thing I remember about Disneyland is being told by an older kid that the people hired to walk around as Disney characters are never allowed to take off their Disney heads in public, not even if they have to puke from the heat. "Get out of my life!" Pam had yelled at her mother, the one time Aunt Ball had stepped forward to the head of the stairs, after hearing her daughter crying. Pam had had a terrible fight with her fiancé, Eddie, who was often seen driving around town with girls other than Pam in his truck. "Well, that's all I needed to hear. I never bothered her again," said Aunt Ball.

Across from the cameos is a photo of my aunt as a child. She has on a white dress and veil atop her dark shiny ringlets. She is posed as a war bride, holding the arm of my father, the groom in officer's clothing—costumes my grandmother made for them. When we visit, Dad, who's the only one of four siblings who left town, always makes a point of saying that his sister got her way because of her naturally curly hair. Then he reaches for one of the bowls of sugary-salty treats that are always there when we arrive, within hand's reach, on every surface in the house.

On Pam's bedroom door is a poster that Aunt Ball says I gave to Pam when I was a child. It is a soft-focus picture of a faucet. In a '70s font, it says: "Emotions are not like faucets that can be turned on and off." No. I couldn't remember giving it to Pam. Aunt Ball peels back the twenty-year-old Scotch Tape. "To Clara, may all your days be filled with love, love Claudia." Claudia was my crazy aunt from the other side of the family who once, when she was a young woman with fantastic legs, gathered up her big skirt at a fancy New Year's party and shat on the ballroom floor. I must have just unrolled the poster, rolled it up again, and passed it on to Aunt Ball. And it has been on this door ever since.

On Pam's dresser is a white bride made from a mop head with button eyes, double parentheses sewn around them like a stressed-out Charlie Brown character. A deer with eyelashes sits next to it, staring past the doorknob. Its rump says "Made in China," is detailed with hard, plastic, undulating hair, and dappled with paint pressed on with rushed fingerprints. It was probably bought at the local hardware store, which sold everything. I picture the harried factory child's finger dipping into the white paint. The deer does not look vacant. In fact, none of the creatures do. They have been sitting in their spots, waiting for so long that they have a kind of dignity now. The waiting dolls. Something like the Steadfast Tin Soldier, you might think, on your way to the kitchen for one of Aunt Ball's squares.

I am an only child, and despite the confinement of Pam's room, she was my model growing up—of how to get out. Seven years older than me, she and her sisters, Kitty and Charmaine, wore red and white, or yellow and white, striped tube tops with breasts in them, short-short cut-off jeans, and delicate gold chains that meandered across their sun-tanned collarbones. They were feathered and blonde and drank beer out of cans by the river. Pam had done one thing in her room that I admired greatly: in various corners, dried flowers hung upside-down from the ceiling, like pretty execution victims, Bluebeard maidens. They made me think of hair tumbling down walls. At ten years old, this spoke of everything I wanted for myself. Each Romantic lover, yearned for and lost, had been immortalized with flowers.

These flowers were mileposts of accomplishments. I, too, would come to measure my life by the segments spent with courtiers who came and went. All my teenage life, I aspired to make my room a boudoir where I would display my souvenirs of Romantic Love. I littered my dresser-top with my mother's old perfume bottles. I draped lace over the mirror. I sprinkled talcum across the glass for effect. Every week, the German housecleaner (my mother's honours student), whose tanned legs rippled in old-school basketball shorts while he cleaned our house, would, to my annoyance, wipe the glass clean.

Now I can't even decide how I feel about a bouquet of flowers I have bought to fill an empty tabletop. It's the word again. Bouquet. It's for those feminine people who say "panties," or that something's delicious when they're not talking about food. Besides, I never know which flowers to pick. Once I thought I'd actually make my own jewelry. All sensual women seem to do this, and I wanted to be one of those. I looked through a bead shop full of sensual women for a long time. I was thrilled each time I came across a beautiful piece of glass or clay, but left without a clue as to how to string it to any of the other ones, though I saw a sign that offered classes for those of us without instinct. I wondered if the infinitely patient women picking through the pieces have taken these classes, or if they just knew what shapes to dangle from their ears and slim necks, what colours would go with their smartly shaped tresses, their green eyes. Their rooms undoubtedly thrilled with the perfect, bohemian placement of accent pieces.

At some point, I changed tactics. I covered the wall above my desk with art postcards, copies of poems, and photos of writers;

overnight, it appeared as though I'd lived a life dedicated to big intellectual ideas and edgy aesthetics. I wanted to be in a photo on that wall, to peer at myself at a desk in a large black-and-white room where there is no concern for the arrangement of things. It is spare, with tack and tape marks at the borders, and me at the far end of it, crouched and working under a badly-put-up shelf of books. I wanted this room to be dusty in the sunlight, and there should be an interesting-looking kitchen off to the side. This image should appear over and over again on the back of thin books with French flaps.

Regrettably, when I squint to get a closer look at the small Me at the end of the room, I'm some guy in a white t-shirt, with greasy hair, who drinks and is too close to his mother. I have no alternative to the howling late-50s poet. If I become a best mind, who will tell me? I have rules: I try to avoid goddesses and fruit of any kind. The size of my breasts has precluded any serious identification with goddesses, and I have never thought of any part of my body as food. Does this make me passionless, I wonder? Perhaps my nose is a little potato-like. I need to get out of the rooms I have made, away from old possessions and prejudices. I throw on a turn-of-the-century tuxedo jacket I bought in a thrift store in Copenhagen and a hunting hat I found at a Kitsilano Value Village, and step into the promising bright streets of my city.

———————◆———————

I wonder why, as I make my way downtown, I am imitating Richard Gere's trademark walk, the one from the past-your-bedtime-movie *American Gigolo*. My hips have narrowed; one hand is loose in my pocket; one arm is swinging back and forth, cool and slow. There's nothing wrong with Lauren Hutton, but she doesn't have a walk. She has a damaged gaze that involves the gap between her front teeth. When she refused to have it filled, it made her famous. She sits in café booths and on hotel beds, looking up at Richard Gere with her gap-toothed, damaged gaze. Nope. At nineteen, my heroes are the young men in books and movies who do a lot of walking. I want to be them as much as fall for them. They are where I'm getting to. They are my Ladies. Holden Caulfield, not his roller-skating sister Phoebe, not friend-Jane, who always kept her kings in the back row.

But a nineteen-year-old girl finds out soon enough that the world does not see her as Holden Caulfield. Despite her tuxedo jacket, big boots, and hunting hat, she cannot just grab a pack of smokes, hunch her shoulders to the darkness, and see where the night takes her. Character is voice, and voice is walking, and you might notice the way she walks out there, but you wouldn't notice the way she talks. You, out there on the street, are not interested in that; and besides, there will be almost no dialogue, since she will say as little as possible to any passerby. While Holden is falling off street corners into nothingness, into existential reverie, she is always aware of the surface of cement. It will be quiet, even in her own head, except for the characterless chant of some vaguely-recalled women's centre pamphlet: walk with purpose, meet their eyes, be watchful of shadows coming up behind; give a little start, mistaking one's own, doubling in a passing car light, for another's so close behind.

Even in barrooms, Holden doesn't get his luck—rye and sodas at a table in the back during a phony piano act. You give a whorey-looking blond at the next table the eye if you feel like it. What could be better? Me, I settle down at a pub table to read a book, and within two minutes, some drunken sod, a poet in his own wet brain, is side-stumbling diagonal over to find out what I'm doing. Like I'm not actually reading. Like it's just an invitation. Like my book is a tattoo or a t-shirt with a band name on it. So here he is, venerating me, spitting a little, with his honourable heart and tales of noble love, or battle, or whatever. He has messed up the first step of Courtly Love: worship *from afar,* you moron. He doesn't get that I am the singer here. I'm the poet. He sees a lonely woman at the end of the bar, and he's a Raymond Carver hero. In his blurry vision appears a little black dress, not my hunting hat. He doesn't notice that I was going for George Sand.

In 19th-century Europe, men were still trying to look like women, or feminine, or whatever—dandies now, instead of troubadours. Poofed-up and leggy, they strolled through Paris with lobsters on leashes, it's said, just to show how much time they had to wander about, how at home they were in the street, how they loathed the money of their parents. The other man of the street was the flâneur: a poet and pauper. This is the type George Sand and I admire. Charles Baudelaire was such a poet. He lined his old shoes and jacket with newspaper and boasted that he could enter and leave any body he liked: the prostitute, the old woman, the organ grinder, the ragpicker. Any castoff of the modern Dream City belonged to his allegory, his broken, beautiful vision. For the flâneur, the shocking urban image is everything, and the trick to catching one is to stay invisible, separate, be a man of the crowd. Some say Sand couldn't have been a flâneur because women didn't have the freedom, then, to wander the streets of London and Paris alone. Without a purpose, a destination, a woman would be charged as a prostitute, beaten for sport, or thrown into jail. But these scholars don't take into account the element of disguise. Sand borrowed her brother's gray hat and large woolen cravat so she could traverse Paris as a schoolboy. She flew from one end of the city to another in the rain, went to the theatre, stayed out 'til all hours—lost in the crowd. Her main pleasure: the sound of her little iron-shod heels beating out a rhythm on the cobblestones.

The slob is blocking everything else in the barroom with his leaning shoulder. His drunken eyes have that eerie unseeing focus, that delayed adjustment, when he turns his head to look at you. Digression, Holden says, is the best part. But I am going to end up boring the reader, unavoidably staying on topic. Trapped by my suitor in Holden's "vomity-looking chair," I'm going nowhere. Instead, I'm forced to over-describe for you the vomity-looking chair itself—the fraying greeny-yellow crushed velvet armrest, hardened in parts by old, better-left-unidentified spills that I am picking at with sudden dedication as my bowed vision narrows to a pinprick under this courtier's breath. Inside, I am stabbing him, like Madame Bovary jabs at her dining table while her life with her foolish country doctor narrows to a knifepoint. Like me, Emma Bovary is trapped by description. Flaubert is like all creepy men who stare: though Emma's eyes *were fully open they appeared slightly narrowed because of the blood that pulsated gently beneath the fine skin that covered her cheekbones. Where her nostrils met was a pale pink glow.* Dear Flaubert, don't be gross. No heroine wants to be leered at, especially by her balding, paunchy author.

Holden can get robbed by a young teenage prostitute, yelled at by taxi drivers, and, despite despair, keep dancing the night away with the bleached blonde who's got the awful voice—keep telling the story. Me, my character lapses into clichés as I edge my way sideways out of the chair, offering virtuous rejection, polite and hopefully believable excuses. As I exit the pub, I fantasize that I am some Angelina Jolie character walking away in slow motion, tossing an explosive device behind me without looking back. The closest thing I have is my PAL: Personal Attack Alarm. Yellow and black, it's fashioned after the once-popular Sports Walkman, and is, apparently, a girl's best friend. So the bus driver tells me. He sells them on the side, when he's not driving a bus. It works something like a grenade: you pull out a little pin and the thing blends in nicely with car alarms and other machines on the street that are shocked by affronts to their personal space.

If I were ever able to complete a night of solitary drinking, whoring, and fighting, I would want to emerge looking like hell, but still good—in the way that says poetic experience rather than feminine ruination. So don't imagine one of those French Auteur Ladies: Brigitte Bardot, a tangle of blonde, naked but for a sheet, the night perfectly fallen in black soot powder beneath her eye. I am picturing the main character from the '60s film *Blow-Up*. Go rent it if you haven't seen it. The hero is a fashion photographer in white jeans and a thick black belt. Growing up, I felt passionate about those white jeans. The photographer wanders London alone, taking pictures. He has the boyish face of a troubadour. His modish, messy hair is dirty blonde, the lids of his blue eyes are heavy, his dress shirt slept-in, his boots Beatled, and the camera around his neck is as present as an unlit cigarette.

I suppose you'd say, what about the Vanessa Redgrave character? She is no Brigitte, but a Lady, just standing there. She has come for the photographer's incriminating photos, which put her at the scene of a murder, perhaps. But she is, well, Vanessa Redgrave—too elegant to be the photographer's half-naked fashion model, too uncomfortable to be a *femme fatale*. Stanley Kauffmann, the film critic, says she's not a person, she's an event—unforgettable but unknowable. In two scenes (of just standing there), she could make the white-jeaned hero dissolve, you suspect. But she is a film still, a photo in your own mind. You could line up all the heroines of European cinema and they would dissolve, like Vanessa dissolves into particles, into the photographer's endless blow-ups: his search for a crime he never finds. Now I've spoiled the ending for you.

So I'll go back a ways, to Sand, Bovary, and Woolf. The hour should be early morning and the season early spring. Woolf says "evening" and "winter," because of how a street is "at once revealed and obscured"—by the lines of snow, I imagine: how things appear and disappear in the high contrast of lamplight. But on a downtown Vancouver street, spring's coldness and morning brilliance have a similar effect. Disguised in my tuxedo jacket, my motorcycle boots, my hair tucked into my hunting hat, I head into the poor part of town, which, a century ago, was the rich part of town. This is the district of old spice stores, flickering neon butcher signs, defunct theatres that became punk-rock venues for a decade before falling vacant again. The glass storefronts that aren't boarded up boast exotic goods and obsolete trades, in old red paint. At street corners, old men lean on their overfilled shopping carts, dreamers coated in sun. I duck down wet, needled alleys to a small park where people score. It is too early for loiterers and passersby, though. Since the city has refused to transform the old Hudson's Bay building into affordable housing, in what crevices and crannies have the homeless lodged themselves for the night? The park's pigeons are busy little kings in purple and green silk cloaks, bobbing at the wet, doughy mess of the all-night pizza joint. High above, in arched stone windows, the occasional hanging flowered bedsheet stirs. I walk amidst the smells of garbage cans, fresh grease, and urine, pass a dozen mysterious doorways, and turn a corner.

An old crusader is standing there—he's using a Crown Royal velvet bag as a purse, and wearing a rose-patterned bathrobe under a ski vest; it's all the same to him. He grips a piece of driftwood, taller than himself, with small brass bells attached. Once in a while, he bangs it on the concrete and sings a song that is indecipherable and lost.

I follow behind him a ways, 'til we come to an entirely empty joint called "The Popular Café." We enter and sit down on a couple of split-open burgundy leatherette stools. A small aproned guy appears, and I order a grilled cheese on white and wait. Every few minutes, my crusader pounds his driftwood on the filthy floor made up of small black and white tiles. But he isn't worshiping me from afar or up close, and isn't out to ruin me, or stand in for my own ruined self. We drink some see-through coffee together. It's quiet. No hero from a cheap gin joint is coming to meet me. There's no witty exchange, no call to endless adventure, no Fall, no crime. Hooking my boot heels, I swivel slowly, back and forth. I look into the soft-edged white coffee cup, at the old clock with its big square numbers, at the charming and neglected tin ceiling high above us. The old crusader finishes his coffee and flashes me a wide smile from his lesioned face. It's a look like one in a million, and my face relaxes to meet his. He's not my Blind Man, my Ragpicker, I tell myself. I haven't done anything wrong, coming here. I don't ask my crusader about street-haunting, or the old Bay building, or what he thinks about entering and leaving other bodies, or ruination, or about the dusty things in his Crown Royal purse, or anything at all. I am a passerby. A man of the crowd. There must be another place to be, I think. I pull down the earflaps of my hat, fake a signature gesture of goodbye, then throw some silver on the counter and walk out the door.

THE CANNIBALS

... poor voyager! For joy
she brings us every morning we exchange
an accelerating series of shocks. We are together
cannibals of her spirit, we feast to nurture
our tired bodies, turning music to shit ...
... You don't believe me?
See her eyes when first she wakes. A visible
tyrant of light yanks their traces, demanding
they stride apace.

— George Bowering, "Summer Solstice"

She laughed and danced
with the thought of death in her heart.

— H.C. Andersen, "The Little Mermaid"

Click Click. That's the sound of his stick on the drum.

The show is long over. The light is gone and nobody is left on the street now. Only an occasional wretch wanders by, who, if he happens to look up into the face of the little girl, coming at him fast out of the dark, raises his arm with a "Hey you!"— freezes in the wind for a minute, then gets mauled by a passing wet newspaper. The little girl continues on, her hair flying about wet in the wind, her narrow skirt stretching taut, making the sound of a bat's wing with each step. *Flap Flap*.

Lately, all the women around Anna K. had been going down, one by one, done in by love. She frowns and tries to commit to memory the defining characteristics of the drummer who'd been playing at the new club, The Starlite, that night. As it turned out, there was nothing starry about The Starlite; it was little more than a hole in the wall—literally, just a small, cavelike room painted red. No place for a boy like him, she thinks, in a noir-ish voice.

Click Click. The drumstick taps nervously in her head. Like a code. The latest assignment, she imagines, planted there by her nameless, faceless boss. Somewhere out in the night, The Drummer's living room window is aglow. Anna thinks of him and his bandmates: happy and easy, moving about in there with their clinking drinks and artsy things, the ironic music they'll put on, can afford after a night of playing their own songs to applause. Their normal, successful, non-assassin-like lives.

Anna woke, turned over, and picked up The Book. It opened in her hands to BAT: *the bat is restless compared to the blue bird, creature of heaven. Its fluttering is uncertain. Unable to glide, it is doomed forever to beat its wings to stay in flight. Because of this, it is considered the symbol of the one bogged down in an intermediate phase of development, no longer on a lower plane, and yet unable to reach a higher.* Dark flight. Ground-clinging flight. Nature had tried and failed, produced a hairy membrane. This must be part of the code, thought Anna.

A failed word, a monstrous wing to music.

Anna closed the book. Before her life as an assassin, she'd lived with "The One True Love," who had led her to believe he was a musician, a saxophone player. This explained why they were always on the move—his saxophone case carried from place to place, but kept in the closet. She kept her singing voice low, so he wouldn't get angry. When they went out, her hand rested lightly on his folded arms. She didn't ask questions when he left in the middle of the night. When he returned, he would unfold one arm towards Anna, who lay curled at the foot of the bed; he'd wrap his long, webbed fingers around her skull, which made her head feel like a ball of white electricity. All the while, he'd talk of a great leap she must make, across a void. Not to worry, The One would say: true love is always best expressed by silence; silence is the best thing you can say; everything exists, finally, in its greatest form, in silence. Etc. And then he'd put her back to sleep as though she were a princess—fanning her slowly with his great wings, or sometimes with the blank, yellow leaves of a crumbling book.

Anna K.'s father, who was a poet, was always telling people that Anna's mother had read *The Odyssey* by the age of five. When her mother was pregnant, another poet laughed and said she would give birth to a book. These remarks pissed the mother off to no end and she gave birth, instead, to Anna—who stayed purple on the operating table for a long time, gasping, chin quivering. When the poet-friend saw her, he called her "The Baby That Ate The World."

Anna's mother and father lived in a big house fortified with floor-to-ceiling bookshelves filled with the most important (though generally unread) books in the world—the kind that needed to be decoded: for example, Georges Perec's novel written without using the letter *e*. Her father loved these kinds of writing games, said they involved constraint that gave birth to interesting accidents. But both parents were almost speechless at Anna's birth. "Oh wow," said the father. "Hello, baby," said the mother. The parents held their future-assassin baby tight to their breasts. Their wordless baby held on.

"The One True Love" was always about to speak. "I have so much to teach you," he'd say; but The One spun in darkness. They were always on the run and she missed her parents' house full of books. Her homesickness made The One jealous, and he told her she was not ready to be taught by a master. He saw words trying to push through her wet, fishy-looking eyes that had become swollen by his monastic silence: *Your word is a gate, call the gate open, call it open…. It is, the one you want.* He knew she was trying to infect his brain with messages like this one. Lines from minor Canadian poets. This irritated The One and he became distant. Then, one morning, she woke to find him at the window, tracing a beautiful lady in the frost on the glass while talking into a receiver in an accent she'd never heard before. The next day, he brushed his thumb across her pretty mouth, said, "Sorry, kiddo, them's the breaks," and left on a foreign-looking sailing ship. Anna discovered that, after all, silence was not always the road to enlightenment. Her mouth opened and closed quietly, like a fish heaving when it's just been pulled from water.

After this, their love became an international affair. This is what Anna told people. While he was away, during the long hours of the day spent waiting, she read 19th-century novels and fairytales about princes who needed to be saved. When she fell asleep, they fell from her hands, and The One returned in dreams to press his cold, stiff wings against her. In the morning, she would go down to the water and sit fussing and yearning on the rocks just off shore—looking out to sea for him while unspoken words tore about her outsides like a gale. Finally, one day, it occurred to Anna that The One was not coming back. Her tongue felt like lead in her mouth. The word and the world seemed to split like a tail, the childhood union gone... and the stories she had read became confused in her head. At this point, she thought, some decide to become victims; for others, it's empathy. Anna vowed revenge, and she went out alone to find him. Out into the wide, wide world.

Anna took the codename A.K.A. and put on some green sharkskin cowboy boots. She worked her way through one European port city after another. Each time she saw a dark figure from far off, as it came towards her, she was pleased the moment she could discern that it was not The One. No, The One's stride is not like that. No, The One's hair is not that fair. No, The One's wings would flap more slowly. She would walk along the water and into the city, recalling how the blue-black of the sea would churn in The One's eyes. "Oh, One," she would think, "where are you in this city?" She had a blister on the fourth toe of her left foot.

Whenever she reached a city centre, Anna would press her back up against the outside walls of little, expensive restaurants, and peer sideways through the windows at decadent scenes that looked like 17th-century Flemish paintings, broken into details by the window's small, black frames. She knew that, in the luxurious colours of the firelight, the hand coming out of the cuff and resting on the mouth was not The One's, because he would not rest his hand on his face quite that way. "A professional like me recognizes these small things," Anna thought to herself. "Can spot a fake." Know The One by a single gesture, a curled fingernail, a ring, the wristbone alone.

Anna left Belgium for Denmark. When she stepped off the train in Copenhagen, she was back in a city she had once left for good—the city where she had first found The One in a storm and rescued him from drowning... or so she'd thought. She hadn't been aware, then, that princes test potential brides for their thresholds of self-sacrifice. Anna walked down to the sea and stood with her hands behind her back, rocking and looking at the industry offshore. It seemed unfair that—after the real Little Mermaid had given up her tail, hair, and voice—this famous bronze statue of her in the harbour kept getting its head sawed off and stolen every few years. She'd heard that, eventually, they had to make a mould of it and keep it handy.

A homeless man came up to Anna and tried to speak to her

in five languages before he got to English, the one she knew. She gave him 1,000 *kroner* and he sent her to a gypsy fishmonger who showed her, on a roll of skin, where The One was living. And so Anna headed that way with plans to enter The One's bedroom and steal his saxophone—or possibly just drop it from the window so that it landed in mute pain. Kill the thing in its sleep that never sang. She knew that it might be hard to find him; he always hid out in the most northerly regions. She imagined a cold, empty hall, him in a severe-looking chair—waiting for some poor, unlucky fool who'd lost his way to wander in and get the surprise of his life. It used to bore her when he did this, as did the long hours he'd spend amusing himself by trying to spell out big words like ETERNITY with shards of ice... but then forgetting what it was he was trying to write.

Anna wondered if hunting down The One would kill the last shred of goodness in her. Her heart was beating red. When she reached the complex where he lived, she thought, "Yes, it will." It was large and composed, as though built by a mathematician. It was windy and the flags were blowing. Six huge hexagons, alike. And the windows repeated themselves *ad nauseam*. The place was like The One. The place was monstrous like The One, and The One might be a small silhouette, arranging and rearranging shapes in one of the windows. Anna stood under a window, looking up for a signal, a familiar sign carried over and put into view on the ledge. The salt in the night air stuck to her. She had travelled a long way and was having a hard time, out on the lawn, imaging how this would go down. It was hard to believe he was here in this city at all, though she could feel him. She could see through his eyes the streets he saw every day. She looked at her forearm as though it were his wing. That day, the sun above had been warm on her skin, and The One would have felt this, too. And tonight was so mild, though The One may be in bed fast asleep and not know this. Anna felt her resolve weaken. She had not heard from The One in a long time. How do you shadow someone who is, himself, a shadow? She walked away down the slope of hill that was like glass, ice.

Anna's little Italian coffee was cold and tasted like shit. Like they used the water straight from the stagnant canal. The One's building lay heavy in a jagged reflection on the brown water—an ugly waterway, probably just opened again to drum up business. The typical row of café umbrellas had an apologetic air about it, for its sudden appearance. Noise and trash were new around the banks that had been reinforced by cement. A modern European canal imitating its own old, twisted waterways. Anna sleepily recalled hearing about streams that once wound across the Danish countryside, but were turned into straight rows so as to not interrupt the farmers' fields. Recently, the kinks had been put back in—for tourist brochures and visitors who wanted authentic Scandinavian nature. It became a problem for the fishing industry. The fish, which had gotten used to the straightened vistas, became lazy and dawdled at the turns, got trapped in little whirlpools. Anna pushed the little cup and saucer away, feeling drugged, off-guard. Though she was following The One, she dreaded spotting him before he saw her: his face familiar, though not exactly life, no; flat, and all princely business. No image in his eyes... *not* imagining her. "I am undoing myself," Anna thought. "I'm about to do something inhuman," forgetting for a moment that she was, already, more cold-blooded than human. Discreetly, she left the table. Before she'd left home, a wise friend concerned with her future had brought up the old saying: you can't step into the same river twice.

At the youth hostel, Anna was given a key with a big number one attached to it. It was quiet. It was early spring and the tourists hadn't come yet. Apparently, Anna was alone in a large white building full of whitewashed rooms. She turned a faucet; she found her splash of water, still there, resting in the soap groove in the morning. She was the only thing moving here. Day into night. She wrapped a black scarf around her blonde hair and took a taxi into town, getting out at a familiar square. It was the one she imagined often, since leaving, as the setting for the romance stories she read, where characters reunite in joyous tears by fountains. The square was empty of people, like an Atget photograph—a crime scene with no trace. She must be doing something wrong; when you are doing something right, there are always humans milling about. All the people she had loved in her old life had left, had built their lives in new cities.

How does your past disappear from a place? Anna wondered. Where does memory go? Deep into the old buildings, swept into corners like fallen bits off city trees. Or does it blow off the stone like ash? Her time here had melted on the docks like seafoam. She knew this city like the back of her hand, all the narrow, curving streets, dark doorways, shortcuts, and blind alleys. But it didn't remember her. The thing repeating inside her was not here. It was constrained in her chest like a stray and piercing note.... But she had come back to Europe for The One, whom she knew was the same. He would recognize her at once. She'd put her hand on his arm and make dinner party smiles and no one would suspect that each step was like walking on knifepoints. She would throw her head back and laugh, pretending to have disdain for that other place above them, above the waves; the "real" world, they used to call it.

Anna was beginning to suspect that, despite her disguise, returning here had turned her life into a cautionary tale—for others to tell in hushed tones, as they do with little girls during their bedtime stories. But *he* was supposed to be the story to tell! Now locals stared at her from behind shutters and she had no one to talk to. A homely man with a long crooked nose and a green velvet frock coat approached her on the bridge where she was casing The One's building. He said he had come to tell her she was beautiful, before she vanished. Am I really the object of despair? she wondered, nevertheless admiring his fine, lemon-coloured gloves. Am I one of those ruined women? She had become a stranger to her own life, become like any other. Her cover, the charm, the novelty of her profession, was slipping like a bad disguise—revealing the monotony of revenge, whose forms and catchphrases are forever the same. She had come to see about a man, settle a score. Now she might be the one to die. She stopped to think about what her last words might be. She pulled some novels from her portmanteau and flipped through *their* heroines' last words:

>**EMMA BOVARY:**
>*The Blind Man!*
>**ISABEL ARCHER:**
>*The world is very small.*
>*(She said at random.)*
>**ANNA KARENINA:**
>*Where am I? What am I doing? Why?*

The silence of betrayed heroines is alike in the end, Anna sighed. Something they are led to, something like no choice at all. Disappointed, they follow and don't understand. Then their dismayed papery faces fall back onto the pillow, and they fade into the blank, final pages of the book. Anna did not want to become one of them. She decided that she should go get herself something pretty, and turned into a boutique selling expensive French undergarments—and knives in the back.

Contrary to popular belief, a stakeout is not exciting business.

When Anna got tired of waiting for his face to appear, she went to the movies. The sunlight burned her, she was so fair; inside, the theatre felt cool and underwater. One afternoon, two films were showing at the same time: a Disney animated classic, and a documentary about a man named Jacques Derrida—Anna was in no mood for something that was fun for the whole family. In the blue light of the theatre, Jacques wandered across Algeria, his homeland: a desert. He came to a little house that looked like it had been empty for a long time and was becoming a ruin, lapsing and rounding back into the earth. "Was this the house of his ancestors?" Anna wondered. He talked about a place he had been imprisoned once (for a few days) with a man who had been imprisoned for years, and then he said that a woman's infinite mourning is something that haunts every man. He talked about many violent ruptures, which Anna could sympathize with: she'd been through a lot lately—lopped-off tongue, reconstructive surgery to her legs. But Jacques seemed particularly afraid of this one wound. There's always something, even for the masters. For some, it's snakes; for many, it's a woman's infinite mourning.

With empty seats all around her, as the man went on, Anna got to thinking: perhaps her life had always been a story. She hadn't been flung, she'd been written into the world. Not even her childhood was hers, not even her mourning when her mother died. They were only the fears that had always haunted The One. Her grief had become a symbol of The One's own undoing. From the time she had been born, under a wave, she'd been the undoing in her father's poems: *I saw my daughter this / morning, trying to walk, & it fell like a vial / of melted lead into my heart, my heart so / deep in my chest*. Treasure sunk sharp into the ocean floor. A stone statue of a prince. Anna's father once said that when you look at life and read it and then write about it, it becomes a corpse. She wished, then, that he hadn't written so many poems with her in them. Before she knew writing didn't have a message, and couldn't teach you a lesson, she'd learned to be the moral of her father's story: don't grow up, it only brings evil, fear, and death into the world. Once you're grown, a piece of the Devil's shattered mirror gets lodged in your eye. Anna had found a fragment that had fallen from the sky to the ocean floor, and she had made a garden around it. Planted a pink weeping willow. She knew she was not like other little girls, shrouded in dark water and playing alone and blind at the bottom of the ocean. Once she was old enough, she tried to escape, swim up, break the surface, and make her way into the world. She must do it now. She traded her song for legs and walked painfully forward, but got caught and was handed over—taken for a killer swimming circles in The One's belly, making him double over. Now she was his childhood fear coming up behind him. Reluctantly, Anna pulled her knife from her boot.

When she reached The One's apartment block, the damp smell of the stairwell came back to her: a phantom limb spiraling upwards. A door thudded on the top floor. The distant sound marked the place where this would end. She climbed up and stood outside his door; scratched her initials, A.K.A., next to his name on the bell; laid her head down outside for a while, then left. Then she returned, a day later. He opened the door. His eyes were as cold as stars in the reflection of the blade.

"I fear you will never forgive me," he said.

Anna was thrown back, fell downward. She couldn't do it. The words folded over her like a wave. She saw blue, then red.

———————◆———————

Months go by....

Anna kept her mouth shut and her big sunglasses on. Back in her country, far from the coast, in the small desert town of her ancestors, in a bookstore, The Book opened in her hands. It said:

And where love ends

Hate begins.

Oh, great. Oh, terrific. But then she remembered the man in the film who said: *reconciliation begins with a single word.* She wiggled the root that used to be her tongue. It didn't have to be a brilliant word, only a small step, one that led you from itself to the next. The words on the page looked like two scratched, Matisse-like lines, branching naturally away from each other like the split of a fishtail. She felt a pang of nostalgia. She had seen a real Matisse, once—the sketch of a woman, smiling with empty almond eyes. It had appeared for a moment in the flash of her light, while she was feeling her way down a hallway of the family she was sent to kill. Anna shook her head. Actually, it was a rare print that had belonged to her mother, but had been taken by her father to his new house and family. Now it hung in the direct sunlight near the door and was beginning to fade.

Anna bought the book. Perhaps she had not been done in. Jacques had said that it was an old Christian tradition—wander long enough alone in the desert and the nomads are bound to find you, and will be forced to take you in.

Back in her own town, Anna spent her days sitting at café tables, drinking little coffees, twisting apple stems—absent-mindedly ripping them off when they reached The One's initials, sometimes ordering a piece of plain-cooked fish. Half-heartedly, she'd carve an oblique message onto it with the tip of her knife, read it three times, then glumly swallow it and wait for magic. She walked up and down the dusty avenue with an animal she had found tied to a bicycle stand, and buried her face in the fur of its neck—hoping it would lead her somewhere she was supposed to go.

Then, one day, his face appeared in the crowd. *Click.* The Drummer. She'd half-forgotten him. Amongst the bodies, people greeting on the street, The Drummer was covered in hanging grocery bags, bending down to some small children. When he straightened up, his face lifted like a big white bird taking off from water. A breath escaped from Anna, but that was all. She didn't want to get caught again. Love might escape through the smallest word, any sound... and reveal her. She twined her legs together and tapped her feet nervously. Desire hung on her in ropes like long wet hair; where her tongue had been, it was pulsing with pain... and now she had no idea what her face... and her eyebrows had turned to feathers.

Anna had been sitting outside the Café Roma on Vancouver's east side, minding her business, reading an upside-down newspaper. An old friend, codename "Little Robber Girl," had unexpectedly passed by; she laughed and said nobody reads a newspaper like that except spies and lovers. Well, how the hell are you supposed to read a newspaper? Anna thought. But her friend was right. She was about as cool as a nonchalant whistle. She had no interest in what was happening in the world. In Romania, for example. She didn't even know where it was. She only ever noticed the fantastical things right around her—and the recesses of her own enigmatic, deadly self. It was only an ordinary Sunday on Commercial Drive, East Vancouver. But the street was an endless strip of lights, colourful costumes, fruits and vegetables to juggle or knock over at high speed, and upturned letters. And she thought she saw a man with a donkey's head amble by. It was the only street in the city, the street where The Drummer lived. "Go get him," hissed the Little Robber Girl, her white teeth big and shiny.

The Drummer began to walk in slow motion with his groceries. Anna had to make a quick decision. She had just retired and wanted a normal life: talk to people more, assassinate them less. She was lousy at the spy element of her job, anyway. She couldn't make up riddles and had never been able to decode a thing. She wanted to tell The Drummer the whole story right then; but everyone knows that when the killer stops to confess his plan to the one he's about to kill, he's inevitably offed himself. She knew better than to be confessional. She knew that what worked for poets also worked for assassins: the good ones survive by (1) not discussing feelings; and (2) feigning their own deaths. All the same, she didn't know how much longer she could stand being incognito. James Bond could never resist a tuxedo and slick hair, not even in the jungle. Spies always look like spies, assassins like assassins—hanging around the park, casually talking into paper bags or their lapels; they can't help it. Even Georges Perec, thought Anna, who got away with avoiding the letter *e* for a whole book, couldn't avoid the obvious betrayal of his own name on the cover. Everyone, even the pros, eventually have to break for the open.

The Drummer is getting close. Anna notices he has long arms and hands like The One. But they do not fold and unfold in the same slow gesture of sleep. They are quick and precise. Make a blur of music, could crack a safe in seconds. He is walking with twelve rolls of toilet paper under his arm, which is not at all dark and mysterious, but what real people do. Toilet paper does not have transformative qualities, Anna rationalizes, not like a hot tear falling on a frozen heart, say, or a kiss after a hundred years of sleep. In fact, sitting there, she had already seen three men pass by toting economy-sized packs of daily household items. They seemed content, rather ordinary, were probably web designers... not like him, managing acts of mundane shopping with stealth, in a dangerous black suit. Probably a cover-up. Enough already. The Drummer is not wearing a dangerous black suit. He is not a Teamster, or a vampire, or even a beast in prince's clothing. She will not float off into the mist or vanish in the crowd. She will devise a way to approach him that does not involve lining him up in the crosshairs. Anna's head begins to hurt.

No. It hadn't been Anna's mother who birthed The Book. Her mother tried to bang out a happy life for them all. She built a beautiful house and put a garden wall around it. But as the father's fame grew, The Book crept in—lay with feigned innocence on the kitchen counter, every morning, a bookmark sticking out of it like a squashed tongue. Her mother couldn't keep them safe from it. Anna was raised on stories of killers, thieves, and martyrs—a telltale heart, a snow queen, a little mermaid... and stories about her father. At night, her mother fell into a trance and sang to her in a low voice about a little girl who slept in the forest because her father had lost his head in a mining accident; and about a queen who walked a bloody tower with her head tucked underneath her arm. Killed for sedition. For years, Anna and her mother huddled before the narrow glow of The Book that was filled with anxieties, deceits, grief, and evil—while her father was out seeing the wide, wide world. Then, one year, her mother drifted away to the back of the page, a rhyme in a green felt skirt, and was gone.

Still, even after this, for Anna, everything was good. She was a little rainbow fish that flashed through her father's poems. A young girl who stood frozen and sleek with water up to her knees in a lake or swimming pool: the landscapes of his youth. Then, one day, Anna's mother died, her husband left her and flew back to Europe, and her father told her it made him feel crazy to listen to her talk. She would just have to do things on her own from now on. Anna sat down on a rock and tucked her tail underneath her. She opened The Book. She saw the little girl there. Laughing and wet-haired, she turned to Anna, smiled smugly, and disappeared.

Now Anna wandered morosely through various cities with 19th-century books and her father's early poems in her rucksack, a silent killer. There was nothing else left to be. She knew that in reality, every fairytale was a story of revenge. For years, she had hunted for The One who had always just leapt over a wall, or escaped without remorse out to sea. Anna thought, each year, she was getting closer. She had been trained to attack: when you find your mortal enemy, don't hesitate, close in quickly and write a poem. *Anna, never read my lines* was a line from one of her father's poems. It was one of an assassin's best tricks, like a snake wrapped up as a gift. *& when / I leave you I will leave you time.* The bite's swelling would be slow, but in the end, it was lethal.

Click, click. Love begins again, with a small sound insisting.

The Drummer. The Drummer was back. His song, planted in her head, was set to explode. A question from The Book ran through her head: *How can we explain the similarity between a man's hand and a bird's or bat's wings except by evolution?* Anna tells herself to stay focused; he is almost upon her now. She can feel her legs gaining strength. This job will be quick and clean—she brings her hand down to her boot—then she'll be out for good.

He has just spotted her. He shifts in preparation for the stranger coming towards him. Is it a stranger? Perhaps he knows her. She is moving swiftly, without hesitation, growing bigger. Her face comes into extreme close-up. He sees the girl's enlarged pores, the lines around her mouth. She is older than he thought, green eyes wild just under the surface of the page. He hears a voice say "Ever." Then, "after." There's just enough time to wonder where the little silver fish went, before the flash of light on the blade, and the deafening noise—like a piece of paper the size of the sky being ripped wide open.

HOW TO READ YOUR LOVER'S FAVOURITE RUSSIAN NOVEL

[W]hat is so really almost painful to me is that I think that art ultimately should be laughter. That's the real pathway.

— **Robin Blaser,** "Excerpts from Astonishments"

RULE # 1: "Against the general rule: never allow oneself to be deluded by *the image* of bliss; *agree to recognize bliss wherever a disturbance occurs in amatory adjustment"*

Imagine a young man at a party—a party that's like a movie full of A-list actors but, somehow, still really dull. Imagine as you go for your coat, this young man cocks you a smile, passes you a bottle of French beer, and asks if you've ever read Bulgakov. This is what happened to me. And not so long ago, either. Even worse, imagine he's a musician who's quickly pegged you as a student of literature. This is why Bulgakov is swiftly inserted into the conversation you find occurring while you lean, half out of necessity, against the hideous rec-room bar in a city which, you've come to realize, is nothing like Moscow. Or anywhere else in Europe, for that matter. Bulgakov, the young man insists, is what distinguishes him from all the shotgun drinkers there. Ha ha ha! you will laugh ruefully to yourself. But really, are you any better? You must admit, his introduction allows for a rare opportunity to reminisce aloud about your trip to Russia three summers ago, before you moved to this god-forsaken dustbowl. You feel momentarily glamourous recounting the interior of the Kirov Ballet as you sweep your arm and quote a tourist brochure from memory: how, if you stood in front of every painting in the Hermitage for 30 seconds, it would take you 80 years to see everything. Or is it 80 seconds and 30 years? You can't remember.

At any rate, he is a guitar player who reads! So why not, what could be better: you are at school. School bores you. Besides, your last boyfriend had not really read books, and only seemed like a character in a Russian novel. Several people, one was your mother, said he bore a striking resemblance to Raskolnikov—tall, dark and gloomy, eyes flashing blue torment, a tattered overcoat. You'd hoped the likeness ended there, but found out, soon enough, that this was not the case. He was a shit, just like Raskolnikov. Axed your heart right in two. To be fair, this was partly your own fault. You've always been attracted to men who look like they've just turned the corner out of some tragic nineteenth-century novel. Who evoke the devastating climactic scene from such a novel just by walking down the street. But at home: Raskolnikov, who makes a great tiramisu; Raskolnikov, who sorts the laundry while you sit down to write yet another English paper on Timothy Findley. If translated novels were allowed in English classes, you might at least have been prepared—known how many crimes and punishments would be involved.

So relax, don't be so suspicious. Enjoy spending an evening with a guy who just likes to read a Russian novel from time to time because he thinks they're hilarious. Russian novels are hilarious, you find out in post-graduate life. You had no idea, too distracted at university reading *Pride and Prejudice* for the third or fourth time. However, when you do finally get to Dostoevsky's *Notes from Underground*, the opening is a revelation. Are there not moments in every person's life where one's experience of a thing separates it completely from how one has been taught to think about it? This was such a time, and though you know Dostoevsky is a writer of somber political and spiritual conviction, like they tell you, and though it's well known that he depicts bitter times for the individual at the mercy of the state, you cannot help but hear Woody Allen when the Underground Man says, " I am a sick man.... I am a spiteful man. I am a most unpleasant man. I think my liver is diseased. Then again, I don't know a thing about my illness. I'm not even sure what hurts." Another example: Geoffrey Chaucer. To your surprise, you find there's nothing highbrow about Chaucer at all; it's all jokes about bums stuck in windows and your wife doing it with your neighbour or the baker. Fourteenth-century smut, pure and simple. It takes a lot more studying to find out gentlemen like Darcy don't really exist. If university reading is supposed to prepare you for life, they should have a course called "The Best-Loved Books of Boys to Avoid." The top three authors on the syllabus would be Georges Bataille, Charles Bukowski, and Fyodor Dostoevsky.

RULE #2: "The pleasure of the text is that moment when my body pursues its own ideas—for my body does not have the same ideas I do."

By the end of a second party (where you and the Musician will have continued to allude to each other's mysteries with shadowy lids and a tossing-about of Russian titles), you will find yourself in this young novel-reading Musician's bed. And now you'll have to admit, he may be onto something. His roommate/drummer doesn't know how he does it; his roommate watches a lot of movies with car chases in them. But you know, like the women before you all knew, the Musician's discovered something his friends don't have a clue about: that there's a strong link between dropping the title of any nineteenth-century European novel and a woman following you back to your bed—even if she's not exactly believing a word you say, even if she doesn't exactly remember the discussion including a talk of Goethe's influence, or Kant's distinction between Phenomenon and Noumenon, or the underlying message that the artist-type is afforded a different moral code from ordinary mortals.

RULE #3: "The pleasure of the text is not necessarily of a triumphant, heroic, muscular type. No need to throw out one's chest.... [P]leasure can very well take the form of a drift."

You could offer his video-renting friends a few pointers: gentlemen, you really only need to be familiar with one masterpiece. That said, you'll want to avoid any machismo: consider Leo Tolstoy's popular *War and Peace*—too much war. Then again, you don't want to come off as a dandy, either: *Madame Bovary* will only have her referring to you as one of her "closest and dearest" friends. No, gentlemen, here is the thing: the book you choose should feature a pale, emaciated (but handsomely angry), existential hero. People, whatever they may say, love a drifter. Kierkegaard's *The Seducer's Diary* is a shoo-in. Now then, throw in any short story that's of the same cultural origin as your masterpiece to show you're well read in the area. In your case, Gogol's "The Overcoat" will do. (Its depressing portrayal of domestic life will deter any question of settling down.) And now you're ready. The main thing is to make it obvious that you have a personal relationship with this book. You should be able to communicate, with a sideways glance, that reading it has thrilled you, that something in you also speaks of this thrill, and that you can pass it on to her in various ways that are not available through academia.

RULE #4: *"[I]n the text of pleasure, the opposing forces are no longer repressed but in a state of becoming: nothing is really antagonistic, everything is plural. I pass lightly through the reactionary darkness."*

When you first open your eyes, you will look back and see that a bookshelf is functioning as the headboard of the Musician's bed. (The rather obvious eroticism-of-the-text will not escape you.) It will be loosely housing leaning and unrelated titles; you'll note that only two are Russian: a Chekhov and a Turgenev. In the cruel and rather hungover light of morning, you'll see there is also a copy of Ann-Marie MacDonald's *Fall on Your Knees;* some apparently eternal tomes of high school English: the *Never-Cry-Wolf-I-Heard-the-Owl-Call-my-Name* variety; and a Mötley Crüe autobiography which is both uncensored and uncut. You will applaud him for his eclectic and honest taste. However, the intoxicating allure of Russian masterpieces that brought you there the night before will have completely evaporated, and rushing to your mind will come a saying you think belonged to Dean Martin: if you can lie down on the floor without holding on, then you're not really drunk.

Well, the same can be said of a futon. And though you are lying next to each other, white-knuckled and barely alive, he will somehow conclude that now is a good time to bring up Emily

LOVE AT LAST SIGHT THEA BOWERING

Dickinson. Is this, you will wonder, a gallant effort to recover something of last night's "polite society"? Or does he want you to know that, despite the present-day depravity, he's still a man of some sensitivity the "morning after"? Whichever it is, it's a definite miss. You are nothing like what boys think girls who like Emily Dickinson are like. *The Collected Works of...* near your damp temple has the aura of an ex-girlfriend—lingering with the unfinished feel of a long dash. It dawns on you that, perhaps, every book in the Musician's headboard bookcase was a gift from a woman who has lain beneath it.

However, here is another thing: men's bookshelves are often interesting for reasons besides the books in them. When you can finally pull yourself upright to retrieve your bra from the dead plant on the top shelf, you will catch a glimpse of a stray photograph: your new lover gazing into the eyes of a girl who looks a lot like Emily Dickinson. You will note, on subsequent visits to his bed, that although this picture sometimes changes positions, it is never put away. Under the photo on the next shelf down are three books mysteriously tied together with pink ribbon—caught midway through some erotic Victorian exchange? Or perhaps with something of the frustrated Tatyana and Eugene Onegin, passionately walking books back and forth between country houses... in the movie version, anyway. And then there's the occasional nameless phone number scratched on a matchbook; a balled-up, half-written verse about some girl with blue eyes (your eyes are green) who makes him twist in the prairie wind, etc. etc.... At night, amongst these things and the unassuming books, you will calmly find a place for your jewelry. After all, the whole point is to show you feel no antagonism, you can go with the flow, whatever...And soon he will feel he can confide in you and reveal his favourite Russian novel of all time.

RULE # 5: *"A text on pleasure cannot be anything but* short *(as we say:* is that all? It's a bit short*)"*

It is important to begin reading his favourite Russian novel early and make sure you read it quickly, because Russian novels are very long and most relationships with musicians are quite short. You don't want to be faced with the choice of whether to finish the book because you broke up on page 150 and there are 250 more pages yawning up ahead to torment you. It is probably a good book and you are enjoying yourself: *you don't want pleasure got from genuine and noble pursuits to be confused with a drawn-out pathetic revenge.* Case in point: a boy who spent six months perfecting a Chopin nocturne because you played it for him on the first date and dumped him on the third. And he didn't even know how to play piano before he met you.

Or perhaps, better yet, reread *Notes from Underground* as a cautionary tale. Skip to the section where the miserable narrator recounts his weeks spent scheming against an offending officer— who has, repeatedly, refused to step aside when passing the Underground Man on the street. Consider the tragic flaw of his brilliant revenge plan: scrounging together enough rubles for a beaver collar to replace the mangy raccoon one on his overcoat... so that he can look classy for a brief but orchestrated moment of collision with the officer. Write "undoing" in the margin. Follow the downfall with a highlighter: after many fevered nights, and a lot of last-minute sidestepping, the Underground Man finally finds the courage to stay true to his course and clashes shoulders with the officer. However, the officer, who has not broken his stride, does not appear to notice the new beaver collar... nor, in fact, the Underground Man himself, who now lies sprawling on the Nevsky Prospect. "At least," the Underground Man tells us, "I have maintained my dignity."

The point is, you want to avoid this kind of dignity. The first step: admit your pathos—that you have, in a move worthy of the Underground Man, spent a whole day combing Value Village for the perfect dress; bought it solely for the purpose of sashaying by your ex at a show so he can watch your ass with regret as you ignore him. But it's time to concede, ladies, that with musicians, every love story is only an introduction to what will never be written. They can only repeat the beginning over and over with someone new, without ever introducing anything new. So start looking in bookstores early, finish the novel quickly, and put it away. Then, if things do end in a sudden, humiliating fashion, you can avoid an elaborate duel your ex won't even know he's engaged in, cut your losses, and move on.

RULE #6: "[B]liss may come only with the absolutely new, for only the new disturbs (weakens) consciousness (easy? not at all: nine times out of ten, the new is only the stereotype of novelty)."

And so, awash with new love, and the new possibilities of your lover's recommendation, you will go out in search of this magical book. You can't find a copy anywhere. One clerk will tell you that this title rarely comes in, and when it does, they can't keep it on the shelf. For a brief but terrible moment, you will imagine the Musician's secret lovers, ex-girlfriends, and the ones he's prepping for the future reading this book feverishly all across town. The more likely explanation is not much better: that his is the quintessential "it" book for this generation of hipsters. Just like a poster of Che Guevara is what all the young men, fresh from their parents' houses, tack with attitude to their new basement walls. Just like Miles Davis' *Sketches of Spain* is the jazz album for every first-year college man trying to get laid via the old-school avant-garde. You were unprepared for this, thinking his love of this book, like his love for you, was singular, special, came from the private pleasure of reader-response. In fact, the book is probably only read now for the author's "punk rock" status—as a man who was forbidden by his government to write. Try not to think about this and remind yourself that, nevertheless, the book is still worth reading, considered by everyone to be a classic.

RULE #7: "[N]ever apologize, never explain."

Of course, he does break up with you on page 150, and of course, you do finish the book. All 400 torturous pages, in bed, eating Pringles off your stomach for brunch. You should have slammed it shut after the advice of the first chapter title: "Never Talk to Strangers"—not on Moscow park benches, nor at backyard Edmonton piss-ups. You never did get an explanation for why he left. But what of it; you should follow his example. That's what the pleasure of the text is all about, says Roland Barthes: "Whoever speaks, by speaking denies bliss, or correlatively, whoever experiences bliss causes the letter—and all possible speech—to collapse." Well, yours certainly had. You were left paralyzed in bed for two days, thinking your spleen had been poisoned by Pringles. "Ridiculous!" you say—when you can finally crawl back to your desk to finish your essay—"it was less than three months." For most of your relationship, you had attempted to fend off Bliss from your desk. In a wretched bathrobe, weeping over your laptop, you tried to articulate something for English 644 about the African diaspora, which you know nothing about. Words like "identity" and "exile" swelled in your mouth until your inflated tongue floated you like a balloon against the ceiling, bobbing you along in perfect time to the exquisite twang of his pedal steel, that you agreed he could set up in your living room... All this because *Bliss is unspeakable.*

RULE #8: "No sooner has a word been said, somewhere, about the pleasure of the text, than two policemen are ready to jump on you: the political policeman and the psychoanalytical policeman: futility and/or guilt, pleasure is either idle or vain, a class notion or an illusion."

Against the previously mentioned good advice about not taking justice into your own hands, you will go to the university library to find out everything the critics have said about his favourite Russian novel. In your head, you will play out the moment when you "accidentally" run into the Musician at a party or show; how, when he asks if you ever finished reading the book, you will sum up its thesis in a few cool and brilliant sentences—like you're reading him his rights.... You will take home three dark and joyless-looking collections of essays. In them, the critics prattle on, sorting through the inconsistencies between fictional events and the life of the author, making educated guesses about religion and politics, breaking down the complicated structure of the novel. Nothing they say sounds sexy enough to fire out at an ex-lover between sips of beer.

You will realize that you are in need of some real advice. Though you never buy self-help books, you will go to the library to find Roland Barthes' *The Pleasure of the Text*. Perhaps it holds the key to the enlightenment you saw on your ex-lover's face when he was recommending his favourite novel to you. Maybe Barthes can teach you to be spontaneous and irresistibly charismatic—like the novel's unusually large talking cat, who strolls around like a person, in a bow tie, boards Moscow streetcars with bravado, and has no qualms about sprawling confidently on a stranger's chaise longue, holding a glass of vodka in one paw, and munching pickled mushrooms with the other. Maybe you will even learn how to build an exciting career like this cat's: working as a magician's assistant, ripping the heads off audience members and screwing them back on, and playing chess with the devil. Now that's the life, you'll think.

As you tunnel through the library stacks, you'll notice, pressed together like stiff British businessmen in the Tube, *five* copies of E.M. Forster's tight-lipped guide dissecting aspects of the novel. However, because your school's "world-class" library had its funding slashed in the '80s, there's only one copy of Barthes' guide to Bliss, and it has to be retrieved from the book depository. Or perhaps no one reads *The Pleasure of the Text* in Edmonton. Or maybe the idea of reading for pleasure is an outdated theory altogether, an embarrassment to be locked away; those caught reading this book are made a mockery of and cast out of school.

RULE #9: "The pleasure of the text is not the pleasure of the corporeal striptease or of narrative suspense."

Once it's been long enough to begin congratulating yourself on how well you've handled things, and not worry about colliding with the Musician at every street corner, you will, of course, run smack into him at one of your favourite bars. The first thing he'll ask is if you ever managed to finish the book. Staring at him—grinning there in the dirty toque he never takes off, his shoes bound with electrician's tape, his only pair of pants— you'll remember why he's irresistible. It's the way with all trickster figures, you'll shrug, recalling your courses in Canadian literature. Coyote, Raven, Guitar Players—shapeshifters who, no matter how elusive, always win back your affection with their irrepressible trademarks. Case in point, the novel's cloven-footed "visiting professor." Though no one is really sure who he is, he is, nevertheless, known to everyone: the Russian newspapers repeatedly mention a mysterious stranger in an obnoxious plaid jacket who's first on the scene whenever a fire or flood or some other hell breaks loose in Moscow. He has a fang that juts out whenever he smiles. He will charm you into doing ludicrous things with him (for the sake of freedom and the human spirit!), even though, more often than not, they result in disaster.

Dumbfounded, you will forget to outwit your ex with the perfect dress and a solid argument, and instead proceed to confess your ignorance of Russian history in the clichés of creative-writing workshops. You did not really understand his favourite Russian novel because, really, you don't know anything about the Russian people of that time, or any time, for that matter, or anything about the politicians and artists who are supposedly being ridiculed by the famous Russian novelist.

As of yet, you have not had time to riddle them out, slowly peel back the layers like an onion, as they say. He will interrupt. "But it's a love story!" he laughs. "Oh no," you'll explain. "It's actually a thinly-veiled allegory. There's Stalin, and some poet called Mayakovsky that Bulgakov despised, and the anti-hero is definitely supposed to be the author because they *both* liked to wear skullcaps." You'll wink and tap your head. Silence. "But," he'll venture, arms akimbo, "the heroine's stark naked for half the book and no one even notices. It's insane!" He is beaming. You will be recalling the magazines in his dresser. The pages with black-haired women on them carefully dog-eared.... The novel's famous naked heroine also has long black hair, so does his ex-girlfriend—down and tied loosely off to the side; and then there's Emily Dickinson with her tidy dark bun. You will feel yourself shrinking in your vintage peacoat that once suggested Soviet intrigue but now just seems bulky. Does this kind of obvious repetition lead to perversion or ecstasy? one might ask. But when you search his grinning face, you will find no signs of corruption, nor even a trace of guilt.

It will occur to you that, unlike the Musician, the critics have little to say about the sexy heroine (even though her name is half the book's title), and even less about her naked witchy radiance, rubbed on by the devil's special ointment. In his guide, Barthes says that people in academia don't talk about pleasure. Instead, they talk about desire, because desire has an epistemic dignity. Pleasure means you've *arrived* and are just happy to be there—of course professors and critics brush pleasure under the rug; it could put an end to the business of higher learning! Nevertheless, loathing your own insistence, you will feel compelled to push forth: "When the heroine leaves her husband for the artist," you will offer weakly, "it's supposed to be like the October Revolution." Your exegesis, however, gets lost in the alarming curves of the heroine's huge body, which has suddenly appeared and is now bobbing naked and shining in the air between you and the Musician, getting bigger and bigger, taking over the whole bar. People have started running and screaming, and the grinning Musician is pushed back into the crowd and disappears.

You determine that the only safe place in the bar, as usual, is the washroom. You turn on your heel to bolt, but in a moment of tentative camaraderie, will yell over your shoulder that the book *had* left its mark on you. "Yes, yes... like a stain of red wine!" you hear the Musician yell back. Even across the frenzied crowd, the Musician's metaphor will sound overly dramatic. You'll expect he meant blood, like from his bleeding heart, and feel some satisfaction that, as you first suspected, the Musician knows nothing about Russian novels after all. However, on an ordinary day a week later, while strolling happily enough down Whyte Ave towards Sam Wok's for some noodles, you will stop cold in the street—recalling chapter 30. The devil's emissary poisons the frustrated artist and his morose heroine with the devil's *moldy jug of wine* that turns everything the colour of *blood.* You were, needless to say, doubtful when the Musician said that the Devil turns out to be a pretty good guy, but when you rush home to reread the ending, you'll see that, sure enough, the same wine that kills the lovers also revives them, rids them of the oppressive city and their miserable lives in it! Together they rise up on black horses and, kicking a dove and some linden branches out of the way, soar into a fantastic pleasure garden where nobody tells them how to read, how to write, or love.... You can't say for certain, now, just what the Musician knows. Which will leave you unsettled for the rest of... well, for a while.

RULE #10: "Texts of pleasure. *Pleasure in pieces; language in pieces; culture in pieces. Such texts are perverse in that they are outside any imaginable finality"*

From this point on, whenever you encounter the Musician by chance, his one-liners ring mysteriously of poetry—and while poetry is a fine thing, it won't help you with closure. So forget it. Keep in mind, like partially burned masterpieces, Sappho lines, or half-written song lyrics in a boyfriend's notebook, these moments linger on because of the unknown story around them. And so, when the Musician is suddenly coming towards you across the grimy Safeway parking lot, shifting his bags full of fresh Alaskan sea bass and prosciutto to wrap it in... and he begins to drawl on about the weather—how he chased an onion across the parking lot during last week's freak dust storm, now he knows what people felt like during the Depression—do not be surprised when (despite the audacious comparison) he transforms before your eyes... is mounted against a prairie sky, a tragic folk hero from some forgotten Albertan ballad! For a moment, you will be convinced that times are as tough for Edmonton musicians as they once were for Soviet writers. Are you hallucinating? Of course, but calm yourself, this is just what the poets call "the meeting of the visible and the invisible"; it will pass. He has appeared, unexpectedly... and so it follows you want to know who the god-dammed bacon-wrapped fish is for, which is to say, piece together what's continued on without you. Consider here the novel's most important line: "Manuscripts don't burn." The Master's book *does* burn, of course; nevertheless, the point is that the smouldering fragments carry with them a persistent (one could say perverse) conviction that whatever has been lost must resurface at some point, tattered but triumphant.

Therefore, wanting to know, you will "drop by" the Musician's new house to return his Hank Williams box set. Unfortunately, he is "just on his way out" to meet someone. Of course. You wonder who she is. He can provide only a dim epiphany, a few flashes from last night's drunken blackout... jumping a fence... kicking a red ball. A child of nature! You'll marvel; you can't help yourself. He rubs his face with his small hand, smiles, raises his eyebrows, and sighs with satisfaction "I spend all my time in here." Cross-legged at his kitchen table, he throws up his other small hand in mock defeat: "I don't even know why we have the rest of the house." Of course not. His charming yellow kitchen is the perfect *tableau vivant*; where else would anyone want to be?

But wait, ladies. Try to keep the whole story in mind. "The rest of the house" is, after all, total squalor. No different than his previous dump, where you endured a dragged-out winter, which should have been condemned long ago: chunks of ceiling falling into the bathtub, no hot water, its hominess spent. The gentlemen, wrapped in scarves, their breath visible, played country music in the front room every night. Stand-up bass, pedal steel, George Jones on a fraying rug. The nightly scene was reminiscent of an NFB documentary: a story about a struggling but spirited community on some isle off Quebec. A charming image to put on a stamp, but you wouldn't want to get stuck there, waiting for spring. Still, this must be what goes on all over the Great Canadian North... to fend off insanity. And with blurry eyes, you reached for a washboard and awkwardly ran your fingers up and down it. But, well, this is it, then. So what is Bliss? A few anecdotes to hold onto like fragile illuminated parchment. Nothing is to be recuperated. Him, cross-legged and grinning like a cat in the glow of his yellow kitchen, with perpetual winter around it.

RULE #11: "The Bliss of the text is not precarious, it is worse: precocious; it does not come in its own good time, it does not depend on any ripening. Everything is wrought to a transport at one and the same moment... Everything comes about; indeed in every sense everything comes—at first glance."

And so, to conclude, the moment the Musician casts you a sideways glance and cocks a smile, you will accept everything—don't kid yourself—the same way you jump when a well-known story takes an alarming turn. For instance: the heroine tearing her clothes off, jumping on a broom, and flying madly away from Moscow—Why not! you say, your heart pounding. However, while you adamantly support the revolution of Bliss, you cannot give up your years of critical reasoning... slowly coming to fruition as you pace the bar's washroom stall: if (a) the name of your ex-boyfriend's new girlfriend happens to be the same as that of the heroine's servant—who *rides a pig* into paradise—then (b) where does that put him in the analogy! But really... you don't think he's a pig. You're not feeling at all vengeful. In fact, you're fine! Besides, a student of literature needs her peace and quiet. A routine. It doesn't work, taking Bliss to your parents' house for dinner; Bliss doesn't want to stay in under the covers and watch a rented movie. But you can't "stay friends" with Bliss, either. And so you will exit the stall and walk home in the wet spring snow with a guitar pick in your pocket. For those who aren't quite ready to receive Bliss, Barthes has this mantra: *I write because I do not want the words I find.* We might as well leave you here, then, with your aching heart, scribbling down your images of loss, while the Musician goes back to his small round table, to cock a smile at a girl whose black hair is spiky and wild in the dark and whose eyes flash electrically with love.

JEANNE'S MONOLOGUE

In sinuous folds of cities old and grim,
Where all things, even horror, turn to grace,
I follow, in obedience to my whim,
Strange, feeble, charming creatures round the place.

— **Charles Baudelaire**, "The Little Old Women"

To the flâneur, his city—though he was born in it, like Baudelaire—is no
home. It constitutes for him a stage.

— **Walter Benjamin**, *The Arcades Project*

ACT 1

[SCENE: JEANNE and a two-room apartment on Vancouver's east side. An indeterminate time of night. Through an open window: city sounds, the stink of rotting dumpsters, the continuous murmur of various languages:

You came into the tenebrous room
like moonlight
and sat on the chair like a pool of light

The walls are somewhere outside the shaft of light. High-contrast separates lit and unlit objects. JEANNE has just torn down a paper lantern from a light bulb.]

LETTER: Jeanne, my love,

[Some people choose to live in this neat grid of poverty because of the architectural leftovers of early European immigrants, which are different from the plastic Corinthian pillars plunked outside popular restaurants pulsing with bass and neon on the other side of town. Moving into places like this, one always encounters other people's paint. The once-luxurious rooms have unwittingly been made smaller and smaller. The edges of the sills are rounded and sloppy, the once-fine details of panels made crude by paint. This is uncareful and un-European. Still, although they are filthy, they are a precarious hold to a foreign beauty.
[THE MAN WHO WANTS TO MARRY HER is being held precariously through a skyline, oceanline, a phoneline. THE MAN WHO WANTS TO MARRY HER lives in a beautiful city far away where the streets twist ahead of you in a maze of longing...]

TELEPHONE: My girl...

[JEANNE is walking around in low-contrast lighting. She's imagining stepping on the individually cut stones that make up European streets, square after square—the many hands that have fashioned them into place. One footstep, another footstep, a blue stocking, a soft pointed shoe.]

THEMIS: Shroud your heads. Let fall behind you the bones of the being from whom you are descended.

[Husband and wife, at first confused, at last found the answer to this mystery. Each covered the other in a veil, and they began to walk across the wasteland. They tore the stones from the earth, Gaia's bones, and threw them over their shoulders. As they dropped to the ground, the stones became human beings: those behind Deucalion turned into men; those behind Pyrrha turned into women. And so the human race began again]

JEANNE: *(ambivalent)* Yes?

[In her neighbourhood, if you look up you can see dates: "1897," and the simple names of businesses, "BAKERY" or "BANK" cut with certainty into stone façades. Far below, under eighteen-foot pressed metal ceilings, are a few malleable bags of white bread and jars of fetus vegetables available to you twenty-four hours a day on crooked stretches of yellow shelving.
[JEANNE is 26. In St. Petersburg, she finds mosques are being used to store fish. The golden onion domes loom over a strange and noble downfall. The neon's pulse has been short-lived, turned to preliminary sketches in rust on the tops of hotels in the centre. Through them, she can see the glorious white Russian nights.
[There are no centres in JEANNE's city—her city began with

three saloons and loggers chopping willy-nilly afraid into the bush. There is a statue of a wilting soldier in a park.]

STATUE: IS IT NOTHING TO YOU?

[Whatever was to be remembered must have been forgotten long before her arrival, and no one has told her what it is. Every time a large hole appears downtown, no one can remember what was there before.

[In the city where THE MAN WHO WANTS TO MARRY HER lives, there is a bank—the usual two-tone, smooth and angular strips of fabricated life—but in a corner, the floor opens onto a stairwell descending into Viking ruins: once the surface of life, now a grey dream under the feet of tellers. Subways have accommodated their lines around burial tombs that gape: exhibitions behind glass, open operations into the belly of the earth. Every shovel hits a treasure.

[The beginnings of JEANNE's city can be found with clues— with the paths of weeping willows, and the oldest paved streets that cave in constantly; they follow the routes of underground rivers, which soften the earth and so determine the spots for unused playing fields, the many required parks that are miniature models for lost bounty, guilty as reserves.

[The people protest over the removal of a car dealer's neon sign on Broadway, because it has been there forever. Instead, they layer a toy store sign on top; and this is as far back as it goes.

Oh, occasionally, in the B.C. interior, someone picks a chiseled piece of flint from the oval stones in Lake Okanagan. White dads show their children the profile of a Chief in the rock face, or an Indian princess on horseback. Young eyes search out a car window for a figure that appears, for a moment, along the highway.

[JEANNE's relatives, who have lived in the Valley all their lives, count the day's totals and don't look up from their jobs in the mall, to the mountain. On summer visits, JEANNE climbs about the ridges looking for an alleged Indian oven, an entranceway into the mountain.]

MAN WHO WANTS TO MARRY HER: How deep am I in you anyway?

[She was never sure.]

JEANNE: *(aside)* Where is the heart... the heartland?

[JEANNE has lived in her city for so long it's become a ghost town. She finds every backdrop street remarkable for its continuing existence in concrete banality—its wisps of garbage, its no thing—while one or another of her washed-out, girlish romances gets trampled underfoot. Nimble boys and girls in silly shoes, sex riding their red robin's chests, stride all over her sets—streets where there are no civic monuments, but pieces

of the past that have fixed themselves to her, like taped Xs on a stage floor. Invisible to everyone else. She is a fading star in her city. Young men always say they will die before thirty-three, the age of Jesus. Women have no such ready marker. JEANNE suspects that many worry they will die when they marry. But no one has told her.

[JEANNE is looking up. She is holding the receiver halfway to her ear.]

JEANNE: I remember... the first time I went to Europe. I was ten. In the square outside the Academia. We had just come out from seeing Michelangelo's David, far up on a pillar because everyone must want to touch him. My first naked man.... An old Italian gentleman, who was obviously there every day, who was waiting for me, gave me a handful of seed and my father put it on my arms and shoulders, and the pigeons gathered from all over the square. I hardly saw them coming, descending on me, covering me in grey—and the grey of the square all around that. I had never felt such a powerful beating, stronger than my own will. I almost disappeared under it. I almost went up into the grey with them.... That day, my mother bought me a dark green coat of expensive wool. It was the heaviest thing I had ever worn. It did not move when I moved; it was serious. Then, everywhere I walked in Italy, I wore this heavy coat and could remember where I had been.

TELEPHONE: A foreign chime.

JEANNE: *(A guilty tone.)* Hello? Are you there?

MAN WHO WANTS TO MARRY HER: I don't remember anything about my childhood.

JEANNE: *(Puts the phone closer to her ear.)* Oh...

[Who is she talking to? She knows her lover's history only by way of bicycle. She pedals quickly through his real ghost town of poverty, owes nothing to it. It touches her with a general romance. It does not really matter to her that his grandfather worked in the harbour in Antwerpen all his life. On the docks, and in a now-defunct factory that has left its children on the streets, without inheritance. A neighbourhood that now has no reason to exist. But does.]

JEANNE: *(Aside.)* Don't think this doesn't trouble me.

...What about when your mother was tired of you and your Action Men and forced you outside, and you sat on the stoop until the sun went down and you could go in?

[Silence.]

ITALO CALVINO: The city, however, does not tell its past, but contains it like the lines of a hand, written in the corners of the streets, the gratings of the windows, the banisters of the steps... every segment marked in turn with scratches, indentations, scrolls.

JEANNE: *(Aside.)* But he screams out like an animal when he sleeps.

[THE MAN WHO WANTS puts his head down, and his face turns to lines and folds. He looks old and, unlike the city, turns into a beast. JEANNE grabs and smooths back the folds, to keep his face from falling.]

JEANNE: *(Aside.)* People shouldn't wait silently for their stories to be told, the way a city does.

MAN WHO WANTS: My mother told that story about sitting on the street. *(Pause.)* I can't remember if it was told to me or if I remember it myself.

ACT 2

[SCENE: JEANNE in the old room of the MAN WHO WANTS TO MARRY HER. She is lying sideways with him in a narrow bed. The room is small, his parents' apartment is small, and full of slips of paper. His mother doesn't trust the Belgian government, and so his room has been made even smaller by filing cabinets full of other bits of paper. His things have been stuffed down the sides and balanced on top. Along the shelves, coated in dust, are children's trinkets that don't look as if they have ever belonged to him, but have always just sat there, awaiting his arrival home.

[The MAN WHO WANTS TO MARRY HER nudges an old

wooden beer crate full of Tintin comic books with his foot.]

MAN WHO WANTS TO MARRY HER: Read out any panel.

[He read every issue as a teenager, as a man in his early 20s.]

I'll name you the story.

[She reads from the panels and he identifies Tintin's adventures in Africa, Egypt, Peru. He draws cartoons of himself, and Don Quixote is one of the few novels he's read to the end. But he is not a cartoon to JEANNE. He unfurls his hand and blesses her head with his palm. She feels her hair turn to gold.
[THE MAN WHO WANTS TO MARRY HER pulls down a paper model of a house he built the first year of architecture school—it has been slightly crushed. The toilet, alas, has been lost; a wall is down.]

MAN WHO WANTS TO MARRY JEANNE: They kicked me out because of my sinks.
JEANNE: What?
MAN WHO WANTS TO MARRY JEANNE: They said they were too big, out of scale, and not even produced. I argued with them. I wanted big, deep basins.

[He cups his hands and JEANNE falls in love.

[They sleep along a sunset wall with a palm tree silhouette. JEANNE looks surprised; she hasn't seen a panel sunset since she was little. It reminds her of a childhood friend she had in Vancouver who was a Christian and lived in a dark basement suite with her mother who had a steel rod in her back. However, she gets used to sleeping under it and the sound of gurgling water blows in coolly with the gauze curtains all night long.

[The neighbour in the bottom apartment owns the rectangle of lawn. He's staged a miniature Japanese rock garden with a fountain, goldfish, and a small red lacquered bridge. In the middle of the yard is a white wicker table and chairs, and an arched arbour (no roses) looking ready for an English tea party. Along the back runs a small Swiss chalet. All is encased by a three-metre-high solid fence. Outside are the half-developed suburbs. THE MAN and JEANNE often run into this neighbour on the stairs and he asks JEANNE about Canada again—he has a cousin there. He tells her every time, and invites them to barbecue lawn parties, which they decline all summer long.

[THE MAN WHO WANTS TO MARRY HER presents JEANNE with soft chocolates, beer that tastes like blood and iron. Try this. Taste this. There are details and no names for things. It is the Europe of her childhood. He pulls her to his dark, soft clothing. Mentions, repeatedly, the bittersweet, something like: "Ah, the bittersweet," then takes her hand and finally they are standing in the oldest and narrowest street in Antwerpen. White and so narrow that the peal of bells at nine vibrates long

LOVE AT LAST SIGHT THEA BOWERING

after the bells have stopped ringing—which is why people come
and stand here.]

JEANNE: What are you thinking?
MAN: Nothing.
JEANNE: Really?
MAN: Yes.

[The MAN's parents have a TV on all day long, while they have
dinner, facing Australian soap operas—eating rabbit, tongue,
and horse. There is a black leather couch and a large white
globe for a lamp because these things are modern. Behind
JEANNE's place setting is a bird that no one ever talks to. It
jumps back and forth between two perches all day, in front of
a picture window that frames the sky and apartments like this
one, a street empty of trees, a below-average bakery that is
always a quarter full of goods. JEANNE sits at the dining room
table with the three others.]

JEANNE: (Aside.) This is not the Europe my parents brought
home in big heavy art books.

[She walked with them through long, vaulted corridors, past
hundreds of thick and oily paintings.]

JEANNE: Mary looked different every time. Jesus, too. Mum

showed me the face of Mary in Martini's *Annunciation*. The golden words of the angel Gabriel coming for her ear. She didn't look too happy about it. Her mouth is turned about as down as it can get. She's pulled her robe up around her, is turning a shoulder to the angel, hoping this will pass for coyness. Despite their polite intentions, both Mary and Gabriel have the same narrow eyes. *(Pause.)* The angel looks like a bully. He is pointing straight up. The leafy branch doesn't fool anyone.... Then there was Botticelli's *Annunciation*. Mum loved this painting. Dad created another family joke. He and I will share the painting. We'll tear it in half. I can't remember who gets Gabriel, who gets Mary. I don't think I wanted either. Dad always teases Mum this way. I go along; tradition. *(Pause.)* I should have told Mum that I didn't want to tear the painting in half....

MAN WHO WANTS: Belief!

[He puts the five tips of his fingers together.
[JEANNE stands back and shakes her head—her city behind her is rolling in and over itself in large toy-like shapes.]

Faith!

[His hand thrusts upwards, the shape of the teardrop running down Pierrot's face, sad little French clown.]

JEANNE: He has always been there. He was there everywhere in Italy. It was what a ten-year-old girl notices. In store windows, on lunch kits. Who is this sad clown? Who is this sad Italian clown that my mother loves so much? She wants to buy him for me, but my father says no, he's too expensive. Porcelain. In a puffed white shirt and green velvet suit. Slumped and elegant, waiting, luxurious and lonely behind the Christmas windowpane.

(Aside.) They get confused. The thrust and the teardrop. The teardrop like a fist.

[This was a difference her mother hadn't taught her.]

ACT 3

[SCENE: THE MAN WHO WANTS meets her in a forest between their two cities and gives her a long, plum-coloured coat. He puts it on her and smooths it down. He looks her over.]

THE MAN WHO WANTS: It becomes you.

[JEANNE sees her hair in blonde braids on the plum collar and forgets. His mother has taken off the buttons it came with and has replaced them with large wooden ones. THE MAN WHO WANTS offers her a ring that has been melted down for the third time. His mother's wedding ring that she had made into a high-school ring for her son, though she was still married. It has been melted down again so it can be used as JEANNE's wedding ring. Just like that.]

JEANNE: Dear God!

[But God has left. All that is here is her own mind, a strange dome in the dark, and her human love.
[She imagines the other country, where the man's laundry flaps on the line outside his window. Faded black, dark blue, and grey t-shirts alike, equally spaced, turn crisp in the Danish wind, making the scent of him—black sails coming into view over the horizon.]

JEANNE: *(Aside.)* Is this life or death coming for me?

[She squeezes an animal consort her mother gave her when she was two. All her life, it has been her oracle. She looks into its cloth face and its expression is her own.
[The phone rings.
[She feels the face of a beast come over her. She picks up the phone. His voice is there; it sounds like it has been talking for a while.]

MAN WHO WANTS: ...getting into our ontological foundation. And that's also why the human illness of getting, materialistically, is such a fundamental alienation. Our ontological methodical elements are sensitivity, belief, will, knowledge. One might call these terms parameters pulsing between and into both metaphysics and concrete conceptualization. They are, let's call them, second degree words. First degree words being: good, god, beauty... *(Pause.)* ...with a very strong reference, namely *activity*.

[The washing on the line vanishes.]

JEANNE: *(Aside.)* What is he saying? Is he proposing? Are these the lines—can this be someone in love?

MAN WHO WANTS: God and the Devil are the same.

JEANNE: *(Aside.)* Who speaks like this? In real life. This is not real. This is not "furthering the action."

MAN WHO WANTS: I have no life, Jeanne, now, but thee...

ACT 4

JEANNE: *(She keeps pounding it into the earth.)* No. *(She puts books back into the bookcase.)* No. *(She is in the shower, looking at her belly like it is a small hill.)* No. *(She jabs her hipbones upwards, imagining something like sunlight shooting out instead of something shooting in.)* No. *(She knows she is not a flower.)* No. *(She does not see anything poetic about nature.)* No. *(She waters the plants, but does not feel nurturing doing so.)* No. *(Lets the plants die from time to time.)* No. *(In fact, she is a swampy mess, she has a lagoon heart.)* No. *(She has put the past in boxes like baby shoes put aside to be lost.)* No. *(Once, she drank eight glasses of water a day after a one-night stand.)* No. *(She likes the bullseye on the Lucky Strikes package. Her*

girlfriend smoked them through the desert in a '60s Impala,
the whole dashboard a speedometer with a red needle taking
you from zero to 120 miles per hour.) No. *(The lovers upstairs*
are noisy and all the women in the building turn their radios
down in unison so they can hear.) No. *(She is not sure how*
"Yes" appears.) No. (

> *But she doesn't say "No." She says—)*
> It's hard.

[Her mother turns out of the doorway.]

HER MOTHER: Christ.

[HER MOTHER spent her own wedding night painting the
cupboards in the kitchen, and HER MOTHER is not a woman
you would imagine spending her days in the kitchen. Once, in
JEANNE's bedroom, HER MOTHER lunged at her father with
a knife. Her father threw a baby blanket over it and held her
hands.
[But HER MOTHER was not crazy, was not crazy. So.]

HER MOTHER'S FRIEND: Marry him.
HER MOUTH LIKE A VAGINA: Why not?

[HER MOTHER'S FRIEND has been married often. The last
one she divorced after six months, after he made her wear

a see-through blouse with no brassiere to a fancy French restaurant.]

JEANNE: Because you are like the woman in *Nights of Cabiria*, Fellini's wife, who plays both whore and wife. Joyful either way. Who ends up on the edge of a cliff with her life savings in her purse, a new dress to replace her tattered white rabbit-fur coat, and her new husband backing away with deceitful greed, no... a repulsion, that she suddenly sees... and so she collapses to the ground. *(Pause.)* And he leaves with her money. Her whole life of whoring, of waiting. Then she gathers herself and her new dress together and starts walking the forest road. And she is suddenly surrounded by a group of young people returning from a party, with party hats on, who are playing musical instruments, and they dance and circle her and, one says "Buona sera" and she returns "Buona sera" and you see she is, unbelievably, smiling again through her tears, and she nods and smiles out to us too, and it is remarkable. And you are like that too, you can return from anything. *(Pause.)* But I am not.
FRIEND: Well, that's Fellini's story.

[Dinner at Fellini's house with Ingmar Bergman and Liv Ullmann. Giulietta Masina, Fellini's wife, loses her shyness and starts to sing. A high, clear voice, like a child's.]

FELLINI: *(Enters from the kitchen and stands in the doorway.)*

I can't leave the room for a moment without my wife making a fool of herself!

LIV ULLMANN: She got up quickly. Did not answer. Through the veranda window I could see her walking in the garden, picking blossoms from the trees. Later she came in again and gave us one each. She smiled the whole time. But when she moved, it was on tiptoe—so that no one would notice her.

ACT 5

[SCENE: JEANNE enters. She walks under the cool arbour her mother has trained in the garden. It is narrow like the streets in Europe; it is like a mother's life that comes before your own. JEANNE is talking to the arbour.]

JEANNE: Dear Mum, I'm afraid I mistook him

  for the beautiful city.

  But I distinctly remember *him*

  grandly waving me into the museum gallery,

  Paul Delvaux paintings on all sides,

  his white floating women with eyes the size of teacups.

  And we ate those little desserts together, in the

     Viennese cake house.

  Shiny wet moulds, in pools of pale sauce.

[JEANNE is 13. Her mother and father are walking along the green, scented path to the little German restaurant at the end

of Garrystrasse, the street her father lived on while teaching at the Free University in West Berlin. Her father is talking with a deep soothing voice and gesturing, until he turns to see her mother far back on the path, eyes closed and smiling, sniffing the trunk of an alder.

[JEANNE reads a page out of her mother's Berlin journal. Her mother is missing her garden.]

JOURNAL: Be sure of the clear, clear space, even if it is desolate, that is at the centre of things out of which all things come. Think of hands in the earth.

[JEANNE is 10. She stands in the centre of a great European city. She stands at the rail of a great river, watching it narrow at each end.

[There is no her here.

[Only the weight of the city. Which makes her feel both grand and small. Let the city do the work; she can wander through it like a child in love with her parents.]

ROBERT KROETSCH: First things first. You must come from a distant place, a bookless world.

[JEANNE is six. She is woken by the sounds of her mother in pain. Even though she is afraid, and only a child, she knows she is her mother's saviour. Her parents' room is eerie at night. She

can't remember ever being up this late. But then she sees it's her father who is trapped. Her mother shimmies quickly up each rung of his body to his dismayed mouth—his eyes turn to a line above him, the archway of the ceiling.]

MOTHER'S VOICE: Little one, little one

is the world really round.

is the Bluebeard of happiness

still to be found.

[Then there comes a time when your childhood is forgotten. And you begin to act in the world.]

ROBERT KROETSCH: You Must Marry the Terror.

JEANNE: *(Aside.)* OK. But never a child, then.

ACT 6

[SCENE: The highway is unnervingly wide. This is the course of their life together—phone lines, highway, lines and lines. They are driving through Poland. The highway was used as a strip for Nazi tanks, over half a century ago. The barrier between them and the oncoming traffic was removed during the war and never replaced. They see enormous trucks turned to dinosaurs in crashes, their smashed heads lolling by the roadside. Which is common. The road has never been repaired, and has been bleached white. They are filled with horror—of

the hazardousness, which is accepted—and don't say a word to each other for kilometres.

[SCENE: They arrive in Krakow, the city where her old friend has lived for a long time, alone in the large house her grandfather built. She calls her bedroom her boudoir and has many bottles of men's and women's perfume beside an old mottled mirror. Her friend opens the door. JEANNE sees again the eyes of her friend, which are like candle flames on their sides. They are traced with dusty kohl, the nub remains of her grandmother's eyeliner. Her friend in suspicious of JEANNE's shirt, which is rose-coloured. They have only a little time alone together, an hour searching after dark in the tiny communist-style shops for a broccoli for their late-night dinner. The MAN lingers in the open air.

[SCENE: They arrive in Ypres. She is confused. There are huge craters in the earth, as though it is the moon, but they are filled with green grass. For a minute, she does not know what they are. THE FIANCÉ has to tell her. She has a repulsive desire to crawl inside one, which is followed by a tourist's instinct to keep a cool distance. Thousands of buried bombs are unearthed here every year—some from as far back as the Napoleonic age. Shepherds and farmers are blown to bits from time to time. This is history as close as it gets; and life seems so real here.

[SCENE: They cross the border to Calais and sit in white-and-blue striped beach chairs on the fine sand. There is a row of open cafés that seems to extend up the entire coastline. An erect *black-and-white waiter crosses the boardwalk to the sand to bring them their slim glasses of beer. THE FIANCÉ smiles in that slight and mysterious Northern European way and hands her a piece of baguette with tiny shrimp on top. It is exactly as JEANNE has imagined the French coast.*

[JEANNE knows nothing about European history. By accident, she reads a plaque that says that Ypres is where the Canadian tanks came in to free Belgium. Is it possible to fall more in love with someone by reading a single historical fact? The city has been leveled and then slowly, exactly, rebuilt from blueprints. This is love. This wouldn't happen in North America—no ruin, no memory. She has seen rows of gleaming crosses and thinks of the rows of hundreds of blue-and-white striped beach chairs, empty on this cool day.]

JEANNE: Just one of those chairs would cost a fortune in Canada and be bought by an artist for his rooftop patio on the west side.

THE FIANCÉ: How deep am I in you anyway?

[JEANNE is five. She has a picture of a dinosaur in her head. School has begun and she's seen the textbook picture of an average man next to a dinosaur, the ratio. He did look smallish, but she had imagined the dinosaur much greater, so big that she would be only as tall as its claw. She had always been disappointed at the sight of great things.]

ACT 7

[SCENE: Belief. JEANNE is in her parents' house, lying with her mother on her bed. Nothing left now but to wait for the papers and the arrival of THE HUSBAND. The bedroom is covered in a wallpaper print of stylized vines. JEANNE's mother said that if she had to be stuck in bed, she wanted a jungle around her. Rousseau's animals stare out from the armchair facing the bed. The duvet and pillows are also a lithe pattern of leaves.]

JEANNE: *(Aside.)* Did she know the rain was coming?

[Time passes. A horrible thing happens. The house shifts. It leans its own weight in grief, and the garden tries to get inside.]

JEANNE: Coming? Coming coming come... coming, come?

[The passionflower is twisting under the windowsill. The water comes in. It soaks the living room and pushes up the bathroom tiles. The grout comes away like clay from a fossil. No one in the house knows how to fix these things now. No one knows how to find a match for the shine, or the deep plum colour of the walls, after the workmen cut a square in the ceiling to dry the insides. It stays open for weeks. A hole in the house.]

HUSBAND: ...It's hard.

JEANNE: Oh no. oh no. You you you you. How come, how comes, how, how?

HUSBAND: I don't love you.

[Just like that.]

HER MOTHER: Oh dear, oh dear.

JEANNE: Mum. Mum. Mum. Mum. Mum. Mum. Mum. Mumm-eeeeeeeeee.

[Back in Denmark, THE HUSBAND runs his finger up a sliver of pure gold.]

ACT 8

[JEANNE hangs up the phone.]

JEANNE: No.

[JEANNE hangs up the phone.]

JEANNE: NO!

[JEANNE HANGS UP THE PHONE.

[JEANNE has a dream that she is in a square in Europe, empty except for her. The buildings that make up the walls of the square are like the old cloth factory that THE HUSBAND

showed her in Brussels. A monument to the industry that was once the city's life force. Hundreds of very narrow and sharply vaulted windows have been cut out of the factory walls—the kind one might shoot arrows through. She looks up to the rooftops circling around, grand and jagged as a king's crown. There is nothing beyond the four stone walls of the square. There is an archway downstage. She is in a womb. It is not a womb. Suddenly, as though by a note of music, the walls collapse in long slices on all sides of her.]

ACT 9

[SCENE: JEANNE sits on the side of her mother's bed, scanning some pages for images.]

SHELLEY: Will Ianthe wake again,
   And give that faithful bosom joy
   Whose sleepless spirit waits to catch
   Light, life and rapture, from her sm—

[JEANNE remembers her mother and closes the love poem that thinks things will get better. The face of the muse. One should never look at it; perhaps it is her mother's still face and skin. Her lovely hair hers, as it had always been. But it burned with love; said 'No' to the false images of love. Like looking straight at the sun.]

ROBIN BLASER: Healing the wounds of these things by

becoming imageless.

ACT 10

[SCENE: JEANNE is twenty-eight. In the car with her father. She turns her head without thinking. Her eyes look directly into the sun.]

JEANNE: Dad, look, there's something wrong with the sun.

[It is a pale grey circle on a pale grey plane.]

JEANNE: (Aside.) Why didn't it burn my eyes out; is there a slow burning to come?

FATHER: There's nothing wrong with it. Don't look at it again.

[SCENE: JEANNE is seven. She accidentally opens the car door on the Burrard Street Bridge. Her hand holds fast to the handle so that when the door opens wide, her face is just above the pavement. JEANNE sees the rough world scrolling by like the silent song of a player piano. Her father, without taking his eyes off the road, reaches over and pulls the neck of her jacket, which pulls her arm, which pulls the door of the car closed. She is upright again, her hands in her lap, looking forward. This all happens without sound.]

[Time passes.]

ACT 11

[SCENE: JEANNE is masquerading around in the cold shaft
of stage light. It magnifies the hair on her powdery-white arm.
There is the illuminated and lonely floor.]

JEANNE: Maybe it's better not to dig up your city's past. Maybe
I'll linger on rumours of an old ballroom under the floorboards
of the Hotel Europa. Chandeliers coated in dust.

[Hers is not a city of no thing. It is a city in which nobody
knows each other. A thousand arms put down a thousand
exotic dishes in restaurants all over the city. We all dig in. For
décor, a single poster that floats "Thailand" red in a fading
green valley. Smiling girls in grass skirts hold white drinks out
towards you in the foreground. The Ethiopian man passes you
your bus tickets. The Japanese girls on Robsonstrasse don't see
you. The swift sashimi knife. The city that is your home is a
purgatory for others. You too.
[JEANNE makes a phone call.]

JEANNE: So?

HUSBAND: Well, you see, it would be like a big ship
turning back.

HOTEL SIGN: HOTEL, HOTEL, HOTEL...

ACT 12

[SCENE: JEANNE is sitting in the Vancouver Art Gallery's café in front of the picture window; behind it, it's raining streaks and big splashes. The muted colours and obvious composition reek of an auteur: there is the marble table, the raspberry and chocolate torte, teal notebook, soft grey jacket; her, looking out the window sad-faced and hardly moving. From this low angle, she is like a girl in a Northern European film. They are always sad-faced and hardly moving. The eye above washes all the objects, including the girl, with a blue lens. JEANNE stands up.]

JEANNE: Oh the cine*maw*!

[Blackout.]

ACT 13

[Time passes.]

LETTER: Jeanne, my love.

HEART: Oh!—

no.

I don't believe you

but,

ELIZABETH SMART: The great rocks rise up to insist on belief, since they remain though Babylon is fallen.

JEANNE: Yes...

BAKHTIN: And contemporaneity, that makes no claim on future memory is modeled in clay; contemporaneity for the future, for descendants, is modeled in marble or bronze.

JEANNE: Or stone. But—

[JEANNE pulls a pamphlet from her suitcase. It's from the Women's Museum in Denmark. She unfolds it.]

PAMPHLET: Besides their children, women have left few material traces; their labour has produced perishable goods. Building museum collections from women's lives implies searching for what has been lost, been worn out or eaten up.

JEANNE: My city began with a fire.

[Vancouver fire, 1886. Structures are built from timber, from the hills of the city. Someone notices that a wall of flame is advancing down the hillside. Shouts of "FIRE!" ring out, but the blaze is so formidable that fighting it, or saving property, is impossible. The only option is to flee.]

ONE OBSERVER: The city did not burn. It was consumed by flame. The buildings simply melted.

[The city, so young and optimistic, had neither coroner nor cemetery.]

JEANNE: But it rebuilt itself. It just moved over, a little.

HUSBAND: I think it may be finally over.

[The news hits her with a bang. Like she's an animal that's been shot in the snow.]

[Time passes.]

MAN WHO WANTS TO MARRY:

You came into the tenebrous room

like moonlight

and sat on the chair like a pool of light

I was too awed to—

[JEANNE stands up in the shaft of light, looks down at the animal, looks up. She is not smiling, she appears to be annoyed, as if there is something more to say after all.]

JEANNE: My white skin

is not the moonlight.

If it is

tell me, who reads

by that light?

[She takes a side step, past the animal, exits through the dark curtain.]

[Time passes.]

LOVE AT LAST SIGHT

*What men call love is a very small, restricted, feeble thing
compared with this ineffable orgy, this divine prostitution of the soul
giving itself entire, all its poetry and all its charity, to the unexpected as it comes
along, to the stranger as he passes.*

— Charles Baudelaire, *Crowds*

*for **Solvej Balle***

Else has been released. Tanja has released her, she believes. Else has moved away to Copenhagen and has begun painting again. She doesn't know Tanja, or the favour Tanja has done for her. Tanja's seen Else only a few times and can't recall if they've ever spoken. Else is in a position of being remembered—by moving away and leaving things behind.

Tanja was first made aware of Else when Rune's solitary figure appeared in the doorway to the kitchen of the *opgang*, where Tanja was leaning, one bare foot on top of the other. Behind him were the dull sounds of the rest: economics students in the common area guffawing over a twenty-year-old episode of *Dallas*. Rune's sudden face was not the kind one could fix on. It did not settle. It flashed back and forth between two extremes.

Later, he would tell Tanja that when he talks to people, he feels like a bird is flying out of his face. Later on, Tanja is given a picture of him with his bony fingers up around his mouth, his eyes bright with a laughter that comes so seldom, he looks crazed. But in the beginning, there weren't any words, though there was something definite. Else lingered around him, ran through him, nameless, just barely there. Tanja felt a sort of pressure when, after a moment of standing there, he pushed surely past her.

When Tanja returns from shopping at Super Brugsen, Rune and Else are standing in the common area—two narrow figures side by side at someone's dinner party. They appear fidgety, perhaps from the beginning of the end. Else's sharp shoulders are up and compressed, her fingers in her pockets. They look away from each other, but are perfectly paired, like Kore and Kouros just stepped out of stone. Tanja has accidentally opened a sealed tomb. The scene holds for a moment, then collapses into sand. Already Tanja is taking out her bone brush to start the recovery, is tenderly separating the arms from the torso, the legs from each other. How perfect they are for each other, how unhappy. Hers.

As Tanja passes by them, towards the kitchen, Else takes a step forward, puts the back of her hands on her head, and arches her back sadly. The fluff of her angora sweater pales her. She is unaware of her body the way angels in paintings are always unaware of their wings, those wonders behind them. Tanja's mother once told her the difference between fashion and style. Having style meant you put on your beautiful clothes and forgot about them. Tanja imagines herself with wings. She would pull them over her shoulders, smooth them against herself—rake her fingers over the folds, finger the joints between small, fierce bones.

Soon came glimpses into rooms. Rune was enrolled in a university program called "Aesthetics and Culture"; he was researching Francis Bacon's variations on Velázquez's *Portrait of Pope Innocent X*. Despite his four-year study, Rune's dorm room contained next to nothing, only a single mattress, a wooden beer crate for a bedside table, and a poster of John Coltrane taped at three corners to the wall; the top left corner arched forward, remained unstuck. But Tanja liked the emptiness, and she almost always liked other people's rooms more than her own. She would lie on the single mattress and stare at the blank ceiling. Bacon's Pope, caged in the faint frame of gilded light, mutilated by the pull of paint over a silent, screaming mouth, fixed itself in her mind.

Over the winter months Else settled into Tanja's heart, the way new friends do, as Rune padded past Tanja's door and left silently down the front stairs—a soft thud at the bottom keeping her awake. When he returned, he would say things about paintings, and films, and nature, over the kitchen table, as he rolled a thin piece of ham or turkey around an endive; and she would nod convincingly until the slow light of morning brought her close to her dear friend with splayed blonde hair on a pillow, grey eyes turned to a door somewhere.

He continued to take Tanja to movies, or make her dinner. During the nights he was not there, when she did not know where he went, Tanja would take him off and put him down heavily onto the night table. Rub her wrists. But soon he began to leave real objects in her room. He would leave his grandfather's watch on the night table for days. It was a watch like your grandfather's—a neat, round glow of gold, well-made like a fact, and it slowly became the axis she turned on.

While Tanja waited for him to come back to the *opgang*, other objects in her room grew hard-edged and sullen—the wastepaper basket and bookcase stared at her. She hated them and told them so. She would go to a café to escape the objects in her room, sit near to someone she had chosen without looking at him or her. Her comfort and sense of humanity lay in the angle between them. She would settle into a book or her food as the other person's chest rose and fell, as their arms shifted; and she would feel as though they had begun to know each other well. Then, he or she would wipe his or her mouth, stand up, pay the bill and go. And Tanja would feel a loss, though she would not be able to recognize them on the street. From her place in the café, Tanja would watch the women go by outside. Often, they glanced into the dark caves of display windows, a world of dark shapes reflected behind their own dark shape. Each one encounters, again, an absence, an anxious dread. Each one wants to find a fluttering shadow of herself, to desire herself.

There came the day when Rune needed some clean clothes. When they passed through Else's dorm room, it was like passing through an exhibit of a lost culture assembled—the living feel privileged as witnesses, but ambiguous about the placement of things belonging to the dead. Along two sides of the room, raw wood benches had been built. No other girl's dorm room looked like this. Tanja could not imagine Else's long white fingers assembling them. Odd, rough-handled tools with dull blades lay about without the calculated placement of ancient tools on display. An unnerving, inharmonious pattern suggested Else was not dead and gone, only momentarily absent.

Rune moved indifferently through the room, around the tools, and the tools were indifferent back. But there was something familial between them, and as he reached into the pile of clean, folded shirts, Tanja could see how the handsaw had cut the sharp line of his shoulder blade, the angle of his jaw. She suddenly felt set apart from them, as though if she turned around, she would find herself amongst a crowd of ghostly onlookers.

In one way, she was relieved. She was a tourist who could pick out any image in the room as a souvenir. On the wall was a painting Else had done, what looked like a compulsive inquiry into the lives of cells: ashen, swollen, pressed together in a mysterious queue. As they left the room, Tanja looked into the open closet. Inside, Else's clothes hung in rows in the dark.

Tanja reached in and fingered a soft orange jacket. Else took shape under it.

Else with tiny white-blonde hairs like frost around her hairline. Else who wrote a love letter about the colour blue, who had a dream where Rune drove his car endlessly on endless streets. Else like a warning, like a parable. Tanja also thought about the colour blue. They had seen the same thing. Rune's eyes. It's frightening, she thought, eyes that blue. No certain surface, no measurable depth. They are ice or they are ocean.

When Tanja first stepped off the train into Aarhus, she was unable to rest her eyes on anything. Narrow passages off the square wound away and walled in the Danes who bobbed gold against pink and yellow painted walls—gods walking the core shopping streets. Same haircuts. Same shoes. Turning their heads slowly, their faces were still with invisible wealth and correctness. What could almost transparent creatures want with cells and crude tools?

On "Blue Monday," the Danish children who had just turned thirteen defamed their golden faces, painted them blue and went downtown, staggered drunk through the streets like wandering minstrels. Tanja had been shopping for the pale clothes, the clean perfume that the Danes wore, when she found herself in front of a boy (surely too young for confirmation) who had landed against the wall of a Super Brugsen. He was slumped, head to one side, asleep in blueface with a beer pinning back each extended hand. He looked like Rune did, the night Tanja threw on his Russian-army overcoat over her nightgown, cycled through the dark to Else's *opgang*, entered the party, and pinned both his wrists to the wall as he started to weep. "What do the police do?" she'd asked her Danish friend, who said mostly they wave people on into the crowd, make sure no one gets hurt. A pretty girl was dragged in front of them, her thin arms wound around the shoulders of two equally slight girlfriends. The toes of her sneakers skidded; her knees occasionally grazed the paving stones. Her head rolled, mimicking sorrow. A piece of her straw-like hair looked like spun gold, stuck in the mute blue plane of her face—the high sky of her ancestry above her.

When Tanja first sighted Else, she was poised on a bike with a basket, in the middle of an empty intersection on top of a hill. She was waiting to turn. Her foot was rooted to the ring road; her long, thin leg was a stem, flowering to the turning sky of Denmark. Tanja's mouth filled with the wind that blew across the country, over the backs of cows, coast to coast. There was nothing to say. Else was a suggestion from the past; but the past in Denmark was not sooty and pocked, as it was in other parts of Europe—monuments and official buildings turned to modern rockface. Instead, its cities were whitewashed and thatched, crooked wood and brick, painters' light through lime-green. Else was seamless. Her loose hair swirled into the sky, made Tanja think of many things, of a neglected thing that seized her. A moment later, Else pushed off the ring road and was not there. Tanja felt her own body cut into an ordinary shape.

Her own body, as it grew older, had fragmented into parts that were not her own. Not seamless, but a muddled inheritance—parts that could be traced to bits of anecdote, or photographs of bodies that had surrounded her all her life. During holidays, these related bodies moved about her, routine gestures made a cage to contain the flutter of life inside her. Every summer, Tanja was met by the same twisted orchard trees with their shrunken leaves, rolling in rows into the brown hills. Her grandmother, in a tent of Hawaiian colour, pinks and oranges, and the browns of the Okanagan Valley, reached over and over her with soft thick arms for jam jars to fill. Then there was her mother, in a slide taken in Mexico. Tanja recognized her own chub above the knee: her mother's legs tight together, self-conscious and bearing down for a honeymoon photo. And her father, Sundays in a baseball singlet, on the dry patchy grass of an East End park, the sun gleaming off the familiar round shoulder that circled the balls back home.

But Tanja wasn't from a small town. She had flown across an ocean. She had stuck her thumb into the road while laughing—imagining the people of this small country, their towns you could walk across in minutes, TVs glowing towards the highway that cut the way through. Who never left, though she could thumb around their whole country in days. Soon she would be going back across the water to her own huge hole of a country, unimaginably big. She promises that when she returns, she'll make daytrips to the ragged greenery that skirts the city and appears in famous West Coast paintings that European tourists flock to see. But most days, she ends up busing a few grayish streets that plot a square.

The summer Tanja returned to Canada, Rune followed her, wanting mountains. He'd always talked about the Sublime. She followed Rune up the Albertan Rockies and sat on a narrow ridge that had looked like a sharp peak from below. She saw the Rockies all around her, peaks like her own. The mountains seemed no closer to her than when she looked up at them, occasionally, through her city window. Touching the gravelly ridge, she couldn't feel the majesty of the mountain. Where else to go, then, if not here? She stayed on the ridge while Rune went on to climb the highest peak. She told him to stay on the snow, to remain visible. Every fifteen minutes, he stopped and waved, and she, on her patch of snow, waved back. It was Rune going. Then a human. Then a moving mark. Then movement became indistinguishable from the shadow and light on the rock. She could no longer tell the shadow from the light. She sat motionless with concentration. The peak broke into points. It occurred to Tanja that she, also, had disappeared; she turned away from the shining mountain. Behind her were tracks where an animal had passed by shortly before. When? The perfectly cut holes in the snow made the absent animal more present than she was. In a moment, the wind blew the ridge of snow smooth again. She was cold now. Rune had her wear her hair in braids and dress in socks of a wool blend that didn't dry easily. She looked like a solid Canadian girl, he said. Her wet legs, the chill at the throat, the shift of the meat at her hip against the jagged rock as she waited. With repugnance, she rustled inside her frozen shape.

In Europe or Canada, Rune and Tanja often stood on docks, one watching the other leaving on a boat, waving and kissing the air, the wave of love looking most true the moment before it disappears. In airport terminals, fingers extended upwards, exalted, just before vanishing behind an ordinary wall.

But Rune stayed this time. Love dragged itself over the daily incidents, murkily transforming itself each time. It mewed about as she and he picked out which meat, turned and pinched the vegetables, separated the laundry: soap and a gentle cycle, days of laundry being done. Else came up hardly at all. Tanja sat at her blank desk and watched a bug crawl up a curtain, turning it into a desert. It started at the bottom, and when she returned, a few hours later, it was at the top, sitting still. It had gone from here to there.

Something about Tanja began to demand space—on the street, people walked by her in half-circles; the seat beside her on the bus was always empty. She did not know what it was they saw; she was only aware of herself looking out. Tanja thought about how people say the desire that makes you thin is not really about the body but about the mind. But she knew it was absolutely about the body—Else's long legs walking away—the body longing to remember what it was before the mind became aware of it, introduced it to time. How it climbed without thought, how it flew its hair, flat-chested to the sun, how it ran everywhere it went, moved easily without judgment in it. "How could you have ever let her go?" Tanja had asked him once.

But it was as though there was nothing to say. Tanja remembered her mother telling her that after her breakdown, she had been put on heavy anti-depressants and couldn't read. People stared at her, stood back from her and told her that she had never looked more beautiful. They compared her to a Swedish actress, to a Vermeer portrait. Her mother discovered that a face is stunning when it becomes unmoving, unmoved.

After a while, Tanja did not see any difference between what she imagined and what she did. The image was enough. No need to write it down. There was not much difference between sadness and happiness. "I've left him." It was like moving from one room to the next. She lay thinly on the bed with her new hair spread out. Else's name ran light under her breath. She had stolen it away, turned her body into a reliquary for it.

Once in a while, Tanja would be seized by the idea that she hadn't known Else at all. Else, whom Rune said was unaware of her beauty. But then, Tanja had only seen Else a few times, and those just after Rune had left her for Tanja. Else had ridden to their *opgang* in the middle of the night and rung the buzzer until Rune had gone downstairs. Something he said had made her cry out once, inappropriately. Then, Rune had driven her back to her dorm and come back to Tanja's bed.

With some effort now, Tanja lifts her arm and measures its span—the forearm is too short, the shoulder too round; she drops it, her hands quiet at her sides. Tanja knew that Else had moved away to Copenhagen and had begun painting again, but she could never imagine that beautiful girl painting.

THE MONSTER, OR, THE DEFERRED SUBJECT

*He had known it long ago, when his memory was intact, when he
had not riddled his memory by using it. He had written about it in other
shapes, but now that it was here again after all this while, he knew that all
that writing was incorrect. Decent, but incorrect.*

— George Bowering, "The Creature"

*I am thinking of an earlier time, a time before
adolescence made monsters of us all.*

— Angela Bowering, "Prodigal"

I walk past a bar window. There's somewhere It wants to be tonight. *Inside*, It's pleading, so I've been looking into downtown windows for It. This is the secret walking I've been doing since I was old enough to want It. Back when it started, I didn't know what It was. Back then, I wandered alleyways behind my teenage lover's house, It howling like a cat inside me. I'd stare through two sheets of grimy garage windows, past the tended garden, and into a quaint kitchen. Between those windows, on a weedy mattress, I found out what a boy *really* was: the assistant to a small creature that swayed like a charmed snake in the dark, had moves far beyond the pawing of the boy. But I wasn't comfortable with Its insistent poking— demanding I think about my insides, suggesting they were ancient, dark and far away. I did not want to be a passive mystery; I was more like that creature. With my arms squeezed against my body, I pretended I was a dolphin in the swimming pool; I jumped out of trees, off tall fences.

The males in the radiant square of kitchen light moved easily around each other, like women do in kitchens; the father's teeth laughing, an Englishman. I was afraid of those men, birthing each other: the father, then the older brother, and mine, the youngest—longing for him; fifteen and longing beyond the soft pink pages of *Tiger Beat*. I would stare with grotesquely bloodshot eyes, forgetting about what would later become gender, and grew and split out of my girl's body. I didn't know what body It became: oil-slicked, bad, ugly, hairy monster stumbling on weak, hooker-prom ankles down the alley.

It has not eased. Years now. Walking, stopping outside of gates. An engine purring in the night. You do not know It, that all of us are secret stalkers. We will sit in the rain for hours behind a billboard just to see you for a moment, slipping from your motorbike, your rainy leather shoulders, to the inside of your house. But we don't want to attack you from behind a curtain, or appear bloody and calm in a closing bathroom mirror, our image next to yours. We get up from behind the billboard, wipe the wet grass from our jeans, go home and put on the music of an all-boys band that wears makeup and shapes its hair. *Girls on film, got your picture.* They all went on to marry models, except one. We put on our brothers' underwear, our mothers' bras, stuff them and push them outward in front of the mirror.

And then we try to find the small, pretty face in the glass again. In *Thriller*, when M.J.'s face bubbles into a werewolf's, over the screaming woman, she is screaming up into her own face as he's looking down into the one he wants.

So I have always walked alleys alone, with my monster face, listening through a wall for the words that might cultivate me, that are contained within the homes of ex-lovers, the ones who caught a glimpse and ran away. Domestic grammar: two cats; a new girlfriend's collection of antique thimbles; over the bed, a chicly-framed photograph by a locally-famous artist; a modern living-room sofa; a girl's small patch of vegetables in the back, shared phone bills that fix It to the fridge, and the boys and hockey on Sundays. We take our cauliflower ears from the wall and wander away, back into the wooded ravine.

In high school, I had a girlfriend who mastered a whole monster body, wandered lonely with it from Carrall to Commercial, in and out of pallid light. She said that once she saw a giant woman with Veronica Lake hair standing on the neon sign of the Balmoral Hotel, a leg raised through the slit of a blue sequined gown, a bare foot poised over the bald head of a muscly black man on a ladder, reaching up to her. She was cut down the thigh, like a fish, the bright red gash women are always mentioning in their poems. Given to them, it takes them by surprise. Men write instead about the time around scars: sewn-up and insignificant markers, her pressed lips. Up the street from this hotel, in back of an after-hours club, my monster girlfriend lived with a boy who did things like shit in the shower and smash her cameras. To avoid having to use the club's washroom, they peed in containers. One day, he threw a pail of piss over her; her in the white wool sweater I had lent her months ago. Hands splayed open, she shook, a dumb violence blazing in her, that she would later express on him with the penknife he gave her. He gave all the women he knew knives; said a knife was the best gift you could give a woman.

While you sleep through every sound, the early morning streets are crawling with monster girls howling for their makers. One drags a garbage can from the 7-Eleven parking lot across the street to your apartment and climbs on top of it. A glum, stitched face appears at your window. Parts of it seem familiar to you: a scar along the cheekbone exaggerates it, like blush. Audrey's cheekbones. Aud was a chic punk who, at 15, birthed a perfect little boy and said it was yours in order to keep you. The real father, otherwise a virgin, managed to escape her and became born again. I tried to dress like her. She was small and perfect like her baby. My heart was sick to see her in the school halls. Black shiny hair, lips perpetually half-parted in red protest. I clanged my locker door. But she was desperate for you, already a monster at 15, and I was calm—It came off like skin from a fish.

A second scar pulls the skin tight under the throat, reminds you of Althia. Her family had a farm with horses somewhere. She danced to pay for college, made so much money that she was always buying you extravagant gifts—pewter goblets inscribed with your name. Smirking, you calculated you'd grossed ten thousand dollars in two years, without working. She used to throw tampons into empty pizza boxes that sat around the floor for days. Or she'd forgot to take them out; once for over two weeks, until the smell was unbearable. One afternoon, she froze onstage at The Marble Arch, her face changing colours in the lights. Next thing you know, she's running naked through the snow, past the black trees of Richards Street, towards the church, and banging on their big wooden doors. You, running after her, for once. The monster face at your window turns red upon finding your description beautiful.

The third scar runs along the hairline, across blonde roots as fine as hoarfrost. The hair is pulled smoothly back into a ponytail, accentuating Else's lovely sloping forehead, the flawless dome I used to crouch under. Whenever she came to find you, I thought of yanking myself up that gold spun ponytail. I have loved them all. Grafted them to me. They have no real history, but are perfect parts—though in me, they are incompatible, a miscalculation. A horror, until the monster asks: who am I? where did I come from?

When I walk past the bar window, looking in, there you are. It suspected I was charmed tonight. I have been out amongst men who wear layers of underwear over their pants, or hang plastic bags of rags from their belts. Some sad Romantic, seeming ancient against the club wall, is spitting his poetry over the throbbing bassline, at a recoiling girl with mint-green eyelids and butterflies in her hair. Now he's being ejected by Mr. Universe-bouncer, who twists the poet's imploring reach behind his back. The glittering butterfly laughs, her stick limbs folded, invincible.

Who are you? I see I've made you shrink, just by standing here. How old are those arms in your t-shirt? I didn't mean to be a monster in front of you. I can't hide all this ragged longing; it goes back too far. Back to the first pulse. Twisted, It rode the edge of my mattress, imagined a honky-tonk bar, a cowgirl on a mechanical bull, or sliding along the bar, her red spangled suede boots in the air, a line of cowboys pouring heads of beer over her in celebration. After, It tried to stuff anything It could find from the bathroom into me. The handle of the toilet plunger, too thin. Was I repressing something? I went over all the potentially iffy moments of baths and left open doors. No. But I was certain something was being kept from me: Betty and Veronica's hard mounds looked more like erections under their sweater sets than breasts; and then there was Ken with his polite hill, like a woman's pelvic bone. Over and over, the excitement of possibility was betrayed by blank stares of skin. These lumps were holding something in, interchangeable alien life pushing through the plastic. That was Its first censorship, when I first knew my moves were being monitored by corporations. I tore down leisure outfits, band uniforms, yanked up tutus only to find the same shine, as suspect as Ken's smile, again and again.

Artwork arrived later in life to alleviate the problem, release what childhood plastic had snubbed in the bud. The monster happened across a book containing a black and white photograph of Jay DeFeo's giant painting/sculpture *The Rose*: a design of lines radiating from the centre, its edges crumbling beautifully. It thought it looked like a luminous galactic implosion, or a fresh compact of face powder ruined by rough teenage-drugstore handling and nightclub purses. DeFeo painted every day, embedding jewelry and wire, moving out from the centre, deepening the material. *The Rose* became immovable: eight inches thick, 2,300 pounds. It became part of the artist's home. In 1967, DeFeo was forced to move. *The Rose,* wrapped in chains, was extracted from the bay window, the painting's light source, by movers dressed in doctor's whites. DeFeo was carried out over her husband's shoulder, her arm extending to the rose, a brush or paint knife pointing. She had to concede to its completion; once removed, it became dry, began to crumble, and was put into storage for 25 years.

I can't hide the monster, who suspects there is something to uncover. Its foreplay is still a buried narrative. Once, hoping to uncover it, It let a boy chase me, like a Zeus conquest, across a golf course at night, naked and pulled down under sprinklers, gently clicking forward. With one ear pressed to the green, a tunnel widened beneath It. It takes a woman so long because she has so far back to travel, you can't imagine, all the way back to Hades on a boat. She wants to dance before you, dressed up as a schoolgirl, a Boy Scout, many things, but also to retrieve herself from the deeps, peeling away each elusive veil. Hers is so new it requires physical ritual.

You catch sight of me through the barroom window, past a number of bodies, and you wave—suddenly awake and airy. For a second, we are young girlfriends, you and I. I break my gait, turn back, ground It. As I lumber through the bar with my swaying head, I become thicker and heavier with each step towards you. You are surrounded by a round of guys, suspicious and having to work machinery in the morning. You are smaller than It, and growing smaller under my silence. Am I scaring you with unflipped hair, unlowered eyes, uncertainty that isn't coy? My monster face twists; my monster heart is confused. To be what you expected, I would have to unzip, pull myself out, smooth my fur down with cream and powder. When I was still just a girl, there was a time when my parents seemed to forget me. They walked in straight lines through our house, were silent behind closed doors, appearing before each other only to smash a window or pull down a chandelier. I knew, then, that gorillas had taken my parents and now were walking around our house beneath their skin. I was certain.

What we say is beside the terror on our faces. You don't invite me to sit down. Why can't we be girlfriends? I go back outside and start walking fast towards the east, telling myself, again, that I will starve the monster, as PJ Harvey does: *Plants and rags / Ease myself into a body bag*; as Ani DiFranco did after she said she wasn't a pretty girl, that that was not what

she did; the way good-lyric girls do, until eventually, one day—
betraying us all, they hang off of hangers on their album covers,
patent pumps falling from their feet.

WHERE WERE YOU IN CANMORE?

Treasure found.
Treasure lost.
Not concerned with what it cost.

— **Martin Tielli,** "Voices From The Wilderness"

3 am

Everyone is laughing at Reed because he is reading out his favourite part about a man who trades his virgin daughter for two donkeys. Or something. Phoebe isn't sure; she can't exactly lift her head. It is very early on Good Friday and Reed has a finger in the air and is dressed in a dark blazer that makes him look like a preacher. On the floor beside his chair in the corner, he's put his black fedora, which he will forget later. The man also cuts his concubine into 12 pieces.

Sean is hanging half off the bed, face-up, sacrificial-like. He says he likes the word *hammered* for being drunk. They try to think of other words but are so pie-eyed—how did it get called that? because your eyes look like pies, wetbrain—they can't really think of any. Phoebe grabs the Gideon off of Reed's lap and finds the Song of Songs, where the woman's hair reminds the man of hanging goats' hides, and her temples remind the man of two slices of pomegranate. "That's... *really* bad writing," says Martin; "Can you say that about the Bible?" asks Phoebe. Fisher says at one point in the show, he looked over at Reed and almost messed up, noticing Reed's temples bulging like two pieces of pomegranate. Reed *had* been a bit stressed—the band's tour money had gone missing, and he'd broken a string that took a while to fix, parents there. Fisher's aunt and uncle too, whom Fisher hadn't seen in twelve years. They left early; what did *that* mean?

2 am

Back at the motel, someone has thrown a tray of food into the hallway by Martin and Fisher's door. But it had been a night of floor-food: ketchup and fries like roadkill behind the drums. Shelly begins gathering laundry. Everyone is suddenly concerned about whites and colours. Shelly doesn't want her whites mixed up with theirs, no way. No wonder, "white" is a dubious adjective, in this case. To be safe, Sean says, don't touch anything but the *outside* of his 7-Eleven laundry bag. Martin declines, gentlemanly—it's only four more days after all—but on second thought, pulls out a mound of congealed grey socks. Fisher is picking through his underwear like it doesn't belong to him. He seems too dignified for road-gaunch; Phoebe hasn't even seen him with his shoes off yet. Suddenly they're all discussing foot size; Fisher has size twelve feet. Martin has something philosophical to say about this; Fisher waves it away like a played axiom. Feet are just for walking on, he says. Phoebe loves tall, thin boys who don't care about their bodies. Fisher claims he came back from the tour in Germany bloated to twice the size "because of all the cheese," he explains, to which Martin asks, "Really? Do you have a picture of that?" because it *is* very hard to imagine. Over the 12 hours she spends with them, Phoebe doesn't see Fisher eat anything except coffee, hurricanes, and vodka tonics in the late morning; a couple mouthfuls of potato mash at the "*Cajun* restaurant," the waiter told her snottily, they "*have* no toast or bagels." But it looked like a regular diner and she couldn't eat blackened anything with a stomach full of last night's red wine, beer, and Scotch.

7 am

No one's slept yet and Martin and Sean have opted for Smitty's across the parking lot from the Travelodge. When Phoebe and Fisher arrive, they are partway through what is ostensibly eggs Benedict—a green-hued Hollandaise. Martin and Fisher agree that it takes special culinary talent to get food this way. Martin pops a nothing-cube hashbrown into Fisher's mouth. They are nice together. The table is rather cramped, the musicians at it seem a little vulnerable, the divider between them and the white-haired couple not really doing its job, and there are babies in swing-carriers on tables all around, and just weird folks hunched over their plates in crummy jackets. *How do they live?*

"This is just what they're fed, so they don't know," Martin says. He says he used to love Canadian wieners until he moved to a Polish neighbourhood in T.O. where there are twelve Polish delis on his street, and now he can't eat Canadian wieners anymore. Even those some would say are the most Canadian of musicians said the night before that they want to get the hell out of Canada. But nobody wants to move to the States, so you settle on the local—neighbourhoods with Polish sausage and good Italian coffee.

11 am

At the show, Shelly's purse had been stolen with a thousand dollars in it; someone said two thousand. After Smitty's, they half make plans to meet on Whyte Ave. They walk past a Cajun restaurant. It says "Smoking Permitted," so they figure Martin will be inside. Martin's in a booth at the back. He says Shelly found her purse and the band money. Phoebe imagines a black beaded purse, looking at Martin's black curls and bird eyes that are round and glisteny. This makes up for everything the night before, and so it goes. Everyone nods. What happens when touring: things lost and found. Reed's hat that Fisher remembered. What's forgotten by one is picked up by the other. Like it happens with the songs, happened the night before when Reed lost his string.

1 am

The night before, Phoebe was picked up and carried. In front of the chain restaurant-bar, she stepped over something, parkinglotkill? into the tour van. With icy fingers, she shook their hands. From the hole in his balaclava, Martin's eyes sparkled and stared out into a starry void. Reed in his fedora reached towards her with a formal but elegant handshake, his skinny tie landing on her. His father taught classical music here at the university. Someone named Sean was curled up on top of the amp in the back. Shelly was driving. She was the road manager. This was her first tour and she always wanted to know what was going to happen next. Phoebe didn't. With her hands together in her lap she watched as the bodies talked, stretched, and smoked around her.

What happened next was, Fisher invited Phoebe inside. A drink in the motel room. A cab finally rolled up, stopped... rolled away. She went with them; they turned and flowed slo-mo into the shitty motel lobby, past the old pop machine, across the skidmarked, working-class lobby floor that would be depressing in another context. The city is unchanging, a stage set to quickly pass through. "Still, it must be hard," Phoebe surmised, walking after them. Each time, bringing life to people at the show in the strip mall, the Earls-like venue. Extracting music, with the jaws of life, from the ordinary day.

6 am

It's 6 AM and the rest have staggered off to their rooms. At last. Fisher is walking around, pulling dry pieces of laundry off things, making excuses for his bandmates. "It's important to gather after the show, decide how it all went, the particulars." Later, when the van opens, you can scatter. But it's a new band, like a new relationship. Phoebe pictures them huddled together beside the dented white van, the cold dawn on the backs of their faded band t-shirts. She walks across the yellow carpet to the Travelodge window, hands on her hips. Despite the snow, the freeway looks grainy and dry. Like a '70s cop show. It'll be there the same, every day. She shrugs. "You come play us some songs, you sleep in a crummy motel room, then you leave." She turns and catches the golden eye of the Scotch bottle that has fallen off the bed and rolled halfway under the nightstand. Phoebe's been in Edmonton only a few months and is already worried. *Music is the orphan's ordeal… wounded kinship's last resort.*

4 am

In their room, the toilet doesn't flush, which allows for an odd collective peeing ritual. It reminds Phoebe of the lyrics from Martin's CD: "and the bathroom just sits / with the memories of a million shits." She thinks it's a pretty good line. Why not. Maybe it goes with the memories of a million beige motels, of which this will be one. Fisher says when he isn't playing, he's painting official buildings. "I'm responsible for most of the government beige in Vancouver," he says. The exact opposite of his red drums, Phoebe thinks. She likes how Fisher puts things. This seems like musicians when they are not playing: they are waiting to play; they are drinking until they get to play again; and sometimes they say they hate playing. But even the nights like this, that seem like work, are better than washing dishes—though Martin (cheek sliding down his fist) says he wants to wash dishes, because then at least you have a clean dish. Phoebe says he does *not* want to washes dishes and is just saying this; he says no, no! for a nice restaurant; she says the dishes just get dirty again there, too. He says, "I've been doing this for fifteen years, and I'm tired of the shit."

12 am

Some Edmonton girls at a table in the front are being real specific: "You suck!" One of them is choking audibly on her rye and Coke during "Take Me in Your Hand," so Martin just stops after the first chorus, says, "Thank you," smiles in a gentlemanly way, and launches into a little rock number about ejaculation. Good. Phoebe's doesn't quite get Mean Edmonton Drunk... yet; this always wanting a New Country cover.

5 am

In repose, drinks in hand, Martin and Fisher look at Phoebe with goofy half-lidded smiles from their matching Ernie-and-Bert beds. "You're both looking at me!" Phoebe laughs. Nothing is really happening, but the moment is perfect, unearned. Phoebe often says, "That was so fun!" and, as with everyone, seldom means it. Well, they are musicians, and music fills a room like nothing else. Fisher's eyes are bright blue. Phoebe's red skirt deepened, her braids glowed, the first time he looked at her—at a show at The Railway Club in Vancouver, two years ago. He wouldn't recall it—lit up and playing.

11am

In the Cajun restaurant, Martin asks, "How did you like the show?" Phoebe tries and fails. She is wondering why coleslaw is a recurring motif in his songs, but "Ahhhh, it was good," is what she says. Martin is crestfallen on the other side of the booth. Phoebe's eyes fall to the two perfect scoops of potato hash in front of her. But how do you ever put words to music? —*words are not quick enough.* A second ago, he had asked, "What music do you listen to?" and she couldn't remember what music she listens to.

Just before moving here, she flew to L.A. to visit a painter who had asked her to marry him. When she refused, he asked if they could rent houses side by side, with matching Volvos. In the hills, where birds of paradise cry out at night, Phoebe, much to her surprise, found herself at a surfer-themed party. By the bar, a surfboard on bricks, a beautiful blonde artisan—who made flat, unusable vases, and was probably sleeping with, or about to start sleeping with, the man Phoebe came to visit—asked her, upon finding out she was an English major, which Canadian authors she should read. And Phoebe couldn't think of a single Canadian author besides Margaret Atwood.

And now here she is again, a troll, this time in a diner booth in Edmonton surrounded by beautiful musicians. She, slow and stupid; and they, like the sparrows who gather daily outside her study window—who catch her watching, stop their singing, cock their heads in suspicion, and eye her up. They know her hands want to wrap around their little chests that are curved so sweetly like miniature models of the sky. She could hardly stop from squeezing. She wants to say to Martin: see your drummer next to me in the booth? He makes a sound that is a thing in itself. Dum-diddy-dum. Self-contained, like a big tidy hole, like a cartoon gunshot right through my chest. I want to make a thing-in-itself too, Phoebe thinks. She pushes the bowl of potato hash over to Fisher, who looks at it for a minute, then takes a mouthful.

12 am

Phoebe is part of a small collection of silhouettes on the cement dance floor, straining towards the stage light like shaky, red-lidded baby birds with open mouths. A torso bends side to side, a foot kicks out, some long fingertips calm a flurry of cymbals. A boy's neck swoops white-throated into the light that's bending over and around them. *You must learn to lose your heart. Let the beat of your heart go.* "You have to try every night, not just regurgitate," Fisher tells her later. "Hope people can hear the difference." But then a server comes up to you when you're having trouble with your guitar and says: hey, can you get a move on? I've got a table that's getting antsy. Probably the Edmonton girls in the front with their rye and Cokes. Paying customers prefer you deliver the evening like clockwork, pain management, stuff it down their throats like a drug.

5 am

Martin wriggles into bed, loosens clothing, flails under the covers and is happy. Fisher stands in a thinking pose. He walks to Martin and folds his mattress over him like it's a burrito; Phoebe perches on top of it. Martin doesn't respond. They can't tell if he's breathing, so they have to stop after awhile. Martin wakes for a second and asks who the hell undressed him; Fisher points out that he still has his clothes on. Martin starts a rebuttal, but then begin to snore.

Phoebe and Fisher go to the Ernie bed, sit down side by side, stare at Martin. The hotel surfaces are quiet. The bottle is sitting calmly on top of the Bible; a clean, nearly-dry sock is draped over the TV. The synthetic bedspread, which was a swirl of sickly-coloured flora earlier, is, to Phoebe's surprise, now a beautiful field widening between them. Out of somewhere, maybe from the hole in the wall, not there earlier, comes floating the poem from high school, the one about two people on an urn trying to kiss: pinned like specimens, frozen for all eternity inside a small woody scene. *Heard melodies are sweet, but those unheard / Are sweeter.* But then Fisher reaches between them, into the field, grabs his discarded sweater and casually chucks it at the chair, and *That detachment / of the rose is the poem's / defeat.* Still, in the wake of Fisher's reach (trailing blue sweater arm), the field is flooding with broken images. They fill her eyes. Anything at all. It all comes, anything!

For example, right now, Fisher looks a little like Mr. Spock. Stop it. As he nervously moves closer, his long shy face drifts up slowly, like a feathered Muppet's. "You have Dr. Teeth eyes," Phoebe says. Oh, shut up, shut up! But this is what's coming! *And how can the body, laid in that white rush, / But feel the strange heart beating where it lies?* Martin said earlier, as he dropped the glass into her hand and the pill into the glass, "It doesn't really matter how it arrives, just keep your ears and eyes open when it descends on you." And you have to admit, Phoebe thinks, Spock does have a certain charm.

Fisher reaches past her, turns down their sheets, and begins moving bedside things into their places for the night, as though they are chess pieces. As his forearm passes, Phoebe sees a flash of ghostly white tree branch. No, Phoebe focuses, these are his veins, bulging, yes, probably from years of hard practice to get out of The Peg. Fisher says he can't play properly with earplugs in his ears. "Now, to play, I'll probably lose my hearing." "Hm. Ironic." Phoebe kicks out a hospital corner. "What?" Fisher's climbing to the good-ear side of the bed. "Nothing." Phoebe noticed at the show that Fisher kept cocking his head to the drums, one side, then the other, like a bird listening for worms. That's OK; it's OK to fall for a man because of irony. Listening while losing it is what shapes his lovely pose. Phoebe drifts off into the sheets below Fisher's nighttime movements, the branch's far reaching, as Fisher continues to worry about his ears.

6 am

Phoebe wakes with a start and wonders if she's fallen asleep. Fisher is perched on the corner of the bed with one knee up. He's still talking. "Sometimes I feel like I don't have a centre," he says. Oh Christ. Phoebe punches a pillow, folds it, and puts it under her head. Fisher seems to have a habit of going on matter-of-factly about music like it's the weather, like everyone does this: daily searching in the extremes of the body. "Well, I guess music must be your centre," she says. He is the drummer, after all. The backbone of the song. Deep-set on stage—a guard with his back to the black curtain. Doesn't he know that *he is so real that he longs for the real*.... Does a centre feel itself as nothing?

Phoebe pulls herself up, seal-like, and yanks the Scotch off the Bible. She knows, "the problem probably has to do with feeling put in place." Fisher had mentioned a recent split—his ex, lovesick, trying to keep him at home with fighting words, just as things were taking off. Phoebe remembers the one. She was often with him, seldom looked happy. She'd come into the bar with the box of CDs to sell, set them up looking like a woman in the midst of a long battle. Sometimes she looked very drunk and would talk loudly in a Bogart-like hat, jerk her thumb towards him—Him, there. Once, she showed up in an unflattering dress patterned with big blue wilting roses. Fisher always appeared the same. His clothes hung perfectly on him; his way of dressing didn't change. Phoebe looked at him. Maybe his hair has grayed a little.

Fisher, still on the bed corner, says he prefers to be alone with the sound. He listens for the music in the room to come back to him, off the wall. "I don't like it when it doesn't come back," he says. The night Phoebe first met him, back in Vancouver at a New Year's Eve party, she kept crossing the room with her drink to tell him she thought he was a pretty good drummer. Finally, he got fed up and said, "Yes, I know I'm a pretty good drummer!" But really, what she meant was, when he'd walked into the kitchen like that: tall, in a long black coat, the room had opened like rocks were breaking apart and falling away. Phoebe scanned the party. Was it possible others didn't see this? Everyone in ironic t-shirts, despite the New Year. Well, of course there was the couch of writhing women. Him sitting there between them like he's blind. Phoebe saw one, in desperation, reach down her leg and pull up her long, soft leather boot. But Fisher didn't notice, and apparently had no need for sirens. This seemed to sadden the couch of women, the kind who like to describe men to each other, have been bred to compete with their resounding walls.

Fisher reaches slowly across Phoebe for his Scotch glass, putting a wrist up against her hip. No. No. Phoebe looks over at burrito Martin... who is, after all, snoring. Still no. She should try to concentrate: perhaps on that pointless little pastoral scene screwed to the wall opposite. Fisher's skin is lean as leather up against her, and it's ticking like fine feral machinery, spinning with skills and secrets, no doubt. Phoebe puts a hand under the soft drummer shirt, to the machine heart. Would he rather come back as (a) a young lover on an urn, (b) a swan, (c) a flower face-down in a pond? It occurs to Phoebe that she is drunk. And... that his thing isn't to go around wooing everyone with a lyre. And! that he probably couldn't come back as a swan anyway.

"You had a single room in Canmore, huh?" Phoebe backs one shoulder into the fake wood headboard. Who would have thought *that* town would offer up the perfect room, in Beige Motel. Darkness, blankets twisting with impatience, fumbling and a gas-station match, lit. Like the girl in the myth, she's in bed with a god she's not supposed to look at. She reaches out and grabs at Reed's forgotten soft-pack and pulls out a smoke. She would bring the light close to see him, too. Who wouldn't? Spill a whole candle of wax on him. "So," she's perfectly drunk, "why don't you sing on the records?" In the van, Fisher's back-up voice left her with the feeling of walking in a light summer dress through her empty childhood neighbourhood. "Incompatibility." Fisher is suddenly awake, and interested in how bad his voice sounds. "A god who doesn't want to be revealed!" Phoebe waves the bottle. "And the songs I sing aren't mine." His fingers are woven together, resting on his chest. "You're right," he says,

mostly to the brown sprinkler stain on the ceiling, "I'm lucky
I never had to decide what to be." Phoebe's seen a promotional
photo in which Fisher is sitting on a craggy rock, holding a saw.
She pictures him wandering the moors of Winnipeg; parents
putting on Paul Anka LPs while he is out there fashioning music
from a saw, like music is just another thing to be cut out of the
harsh Manitoba landscape. Phoebe has never been to Winnipeg.
"I've read that people can turn violent or numb if they can't
make art," Phoebe says, with smoke coming out of her mouth.
He nods; he knows; "but there's something's missing with just
music." Words. She has words. "Where were you in Canmore?"
he says, smiling. She puts the open bottle onto the pillow and
falls to the mattress. "There are only 12 hours together," he
points out, exasperated. "You have to do everything you want in
a short time." She crushes the red end of the cigarette inside the
Scotch cap. That's true.

8 am

Pushed to a quarter of the bed, the sheet yanked off her, Phoebe
reluctantly listens to Martin and Fisher snoring. Contrapuntal,
even in sleep. The show's coming back to them in drunken
dreams, and is drilling through her skull. Phoebe leans on an
elbow with a hand under her bangs; the other she passes over
Fisher's short, thick hair. His head is like the back of a hedgehog.
In Northern Europe, they scurry around, wild. She came across
one once, busy on its moonlit path. It froze still and curled up

when she stopped to look at it. *Trying to touch him, she touches sleep.* Maybe Fisher will wake up soon. She lies back down again, carefully. Musicians still need the real world sometimes, don't they?

9 am

A dull light under a stiff curtain. They wake up in a room in the middle of a parking lot to the sound of someone cleaning up the broken cup on the other side of the door. Fisher's stirring. "There are people working!" He's appalled. Phoebe sleepily searches for something to explain the people. "They're just doing their job." The front desk begins to call. The front desk begins to knock at the door, threatening an extra night's charge. "Front desk! Front desk!" Fisher mimics. Martin is standing with his curls askew, hands up, baffled as always. "We're in a parking lot in the middle of nowhere; what could they possibly want with our room?" Big-front-desk-parking-lot-convention. Martin flops down again, bats at the remote that's chained to the TV. They don't let you get away with anything. He slingshots it behind the TV. There, that's better. Wraps the sheet around him like the movies, "Ta-da!" and hops, stumbles to the bathroom. With Martin finally out, Phoebe thinks she'll pull Fisher back into their starched-clean cocoon. *The memory of whiteness*; but Fisher's already shaken off the sheet and is moving around the wreckage of the room.

He sits down in Reed's pulpit-chair from the night before,

on top of some balled-up covers. With his hands on his knees, he looks at the carpet. Hungover and heavyfaced in the beam of bathroom light. Phoebe wonders how you can go on, timing life to music, without becoming exhausted by the constant, rapturous whathaveyou. Maybe you just don't bother with the mornings after. "I don't really know how to talk after a night like this," Fisher says. "I don't do this normally, what do people say?" Phoebe shakes her head and pulls up her green cords; if he doesn't know the road-fuck lexicon, she certainly doesn't. She thought last night could be easily lifted, snuck out like the Bible or a tiny shampoo—kept safe amongst his things all tour. She had not anticipated this sudden closeness—like when someone's baby is dropped in your lap and you can smell the baby-smell of its head; or like when an acquaintance's dog, with cute short legs, leans up against you in the back seat of a car and looks up at you.

10 am

They have 12 hours together. Some of it is sleep; some is walking around in the dusty wind. They spend some of the morning in the lobbies of motels, trying to locate bandmates and cabs. "Edmonton is a suburb of itself," Phoebe says; she likes walking around it with him. Empty lots, mounds of dirt, wide intersections. Fisher says, "I think I'd better keep moving." A bar that's open. They go in for juice. It exits onto a courtyard of palm trees and a fountain. A far-flung imitation of the tropics? Where the hell is this? A strange enclosure. "You know, if I weren't going to Russia in two days." Hmm, yes. Russia. Oh God. Phoebe pulls her coat across her, follows him back through the bar. In the dark interior, old men appear in the flashing light of the VLTs— to tell you there's chance and endless dry hope. Fisher moves quickly out onto the street again and shakes his head. Phoebe tries to fall into step with him because this is not her town either, she is moving too. You have to live a magical life, right?

1 pm

12 easy pieces. Cut and traded. It is and isn't a rock star thing. Caught inside the cliché, the drunk sleeplessness, is a lullaby— the endless song against waking up. Phoebe recalls Fisher's arm. A white birch branch. How it lay asleep while she had pressed down on it with her finger, looking for a valve or something. But it was just a lovely human arm. The hours have fallen from it in a bright jumble, to the floor beneath the kitchen table where she sits cross-legged in her skirt.

She imagines them moving on to Calgary, all stuffed into the back of the tour van like it's a little stage. Little tin wind-up men, instruments shiny and ready. And she's like one of those women left behind with a kerchief, waving to the dust of car wheels. She's a vertical line on the prairie that's widening around her with the van moving south. In Phoebe's head, the middle of the country is a blank. No walls for the music to bounce off of. There is just her own rush of words that she mistook for his sound coming back. Him. There. A body on the page to return to.

With a flick of her skirt, Phoebe steps out from behind the table. Done. As she walks to the living room, a tap of stealthy cymbals fades in, pads along close behind. She turns on the TV and drops in front of *The Nature of Things*. A lion looks up. "An adolescent lion preys on what's warmest and softest," says David Suzuki, wilderness expert. In fact, one is just moments away from chomping down on a baby deer. You can tell by the sweet concentration on the young lion's face that it's innocent to its own violence. Drum rolls sharp and light. The jaws gently open; the teeth brush over the snow-white down—then a swift tug rips the belly open. "Curtains," Phoebe mutters. Oh well, survival of the fittest and all. She gets up, goes to the bathroom, and fiddles with a barrette. Nevermind. Embarrassed, she had waited for the teenage girls (who'd bought the band shooters all night) to finish their pitch. When she'd walked tentatively up to the stage, Fisher crossed it right away, looked at her and crouched down.

12 pm

Phoebe stands with them outside the Cajun restaurant on Whyte, waiting for Shelly to bring round the van. The avenue where she lives: long, leafless, trailing off somewhere—to an overpass stamped with the words "Designated Gray Space." Maybe official, maybe a joke. Martin was right; Phoebe looks at the salt-worn Edmonton sidewalk. In this Age, the level of rejoicing in the Song of Songs just makes for bad writing. Teeth are *not* like rows of shiny sheep in a rolling field. The world in the song is long gone. Still, it's nice that the ancient singer can't seem to help himself: looking around at whatever is growing nearby in the field, he grabs it and hangs it all on his lover's body. Until the body disappears under it and becomes the whole green world.

The van is there. Phoebe puts her forehead against Fisher's lapel. He is playing again tonight, somewhere else. She takes her head away. *Let sounds be sounds.* Live and escaping. Fisher steps up backwards and disappears into the mouth of the van. She turns to go, a tentative path back towards her apartment. What will she do? There's a café by her house. The walls are painted with deer and other forest animals, and the ceiling is a hanging garden of plastic flowers. The other day, she got talking to one of the sisters who own it. It turns out they'd seen the same documentary about Aran, a group of small islands in the choppy waters off Ireland. "Because, even though the island is made up entirely of rock, people live there." The sister has a big smile and wears a silk flower in her dusty brown hair. She reminds Phoebe of Loretta Lynn, in her baby blue dress with white trim that she wears over her jeans. "They have to drag seaweed all the way from the shore to the top of the island, and stick it down the cracks of the rock," except the sister also wears big winter boots. "Those people have to make their own soil just to live. It's crazy!" she smiled.

Phoebe thinks about Fisher moving across Canada. *I went*

to the forest, to the living wood, to get a potent branch... a potent branch I got. It quivers in her fist. The colour in her is green again. The snow on the side street is brilliant in the sun. She's the girl after the show in Edmonton. On her way to the café, Phoebe remembers a story her father told her, about being at a jazz club in Montreal in the '60s, listening to Rashied Ali going so hard on the drums that he lost a drumstick, and how her father, in the first row, caught it on one bounce and handed it right back to him. He hardly missed a beat. Phoebe's at the light when the tour van turns the corner to the highway. 5 ghostly hands wave from inside the dark cab; 1 waves back from the sidewalk, throws them a kiss.

THE SITTER

Her commitment was to the far away.
Such fidelity was sustainable because of two things:
a deep pictoral scepticism and a highly disciplined patience . . .
. . . scepticism tells her that painting can never get the better of appearances.
Painting is always behind.
But the difference is that, once finished, the image remains fixed.
This is why the image has to be full—
not of resemblance but of searching.
All tricks wear thin.
Only what comes unasked has a hope.

— **John Berger**, "Penelope"

why did you turn?
why did you glance back?
why did you hesitate for that moment?

. . .

what was it that crossed my face
with the light from yours

— **H.D.**, "Eurydice"

The internet is not the sea.

Eira is poised on a chair and staring into a square of light. It looks like she's been fixed this way for some time, her sunglasses pushed to the top of head, though it's the middle of the night now. She could be a photograph, apart from her eyes that are slowly getting wet, like the rim of a skirt wading in.

"Deep immersion." It's a term used to describe young men lost in gaming adventure. To Eira, it sounds more like the state of some Homeric woman whose gaze falls on the horizon after she says goodbye to her beloved—a sailor who sets foot confidently into his boat and pushes off into God knows where. Whenever Eira comes across this kind of scene in a period-piece film, she leans back from the screen, incredulous and uncomfortable on behalf of those men and women from the past; how can they stand always being soaked through at the leg? Walking around unbothered by boots full of water? Too much time spent in that indeterminate space between land and open sea, pushing things out or dragging them in, in a tradition that's now something only for history and songs, what with today's abstract methods of trading. In her own time, there are people Eira knows who can't even stand the idea of getting wet.

On Protection Island, a small, pretty, car-less island off the west coast, Eira has been sitting day after day in a large, octagonal room. Behind her computer, through the bay window, is the sea in triptych, taking up the whole west side of the kitchen. At the moment, though, the sea is replaced by her reflection. Snow drops onto formless rocks, into water she can't see.

The internet is not the Sea. Eira is alone and the line repeats itself. She shrinks the photos and rises from the warm glow, rubbing her legs and arms the way a painter's model does after a long sitting. She grabs a thin wool blanket on her way to the window, which is alarmingly black, framed by some kind of blonde wood. Eira would even say frightening, but assumes this is because she's not used to it—that all people from the city must feel unsettled when they suddenly find themselves in the middle of nature with nothing out there but the imagined ocean. The heart of night. She puts her forehead onto the cold glass; her reflection leans in to meet her.

The proper women from the past, with their dirty hems, turned inland and lit candles in the windows of crude houses on the shore and prayed. Then they climbed up to their widow's walks and commenced a lifetime of staring across open darkness. Perhaps their men had fallen in love with wenches in foreign ports, moved to island homes and taken up new wives, were fighting a long war, been promoted somewhere in the colony, or, been swallowed up by sea monsters... perhaps they would one day return. One could never be sure; many of the world's stories Eira has read rely on this uncertainty—Penelope and Odysseus, Eurydice and Orpheus—the test of a heroine's undying love is hope and infinite patience.

But *hope is a long affair.* Mankind had gotten tired of it; impatience had won out. Nowadays, nobody waits for a ship to appear on a horizon—a slow revelation of an image through mist, the gradual sign of a far-off light. The bright expanse of screen has put an end to distance. The search is quick. Barely a search. From anywhere, even a small island off the Pacific coast, an old beloved reappears suddenly, when asked for, his face heroic under a company logo, the log of a life in sidebar, inviting one to enquire about his company. And she... the long-lost lover who retrieves him... doesn't enquire. The sea, like the internet, is navigated with a false premise. As if new routes out are ever paths to connect people, and not the way to chart loss.

Eira had met Matthew years ago, in a night course on Canadian literature. Their university was on top of a mountain and often described as a grey and brutal fortress. But Eira's father had been an English professor there for thirty years; she had known it since childhood and found the wet, porous cement and the hard, fixed lines comforting. In the quadrangle, beneath the long downward-looking eyes of the offices, Eira killed the hours waiting for her father by wading up to her knees in the expansive courtyard pond. Face to the water, she pushed her toes through the muck until, through a cloud, the gleam of coin appeared. Summer after summer, she glided around the glassy rectangle. Then, one day, an enraged white-haired professor stopped on the bridge and told her to get out, and she did, and she never went back in.

Eira told Matthew this story during one of their breaks, when they climbed up to the flat roof of the quad and walked along the maze of boardwalk made of wet cedar. They settled on the edge, sparked up a joint, and looked northwest over the trees towards the foggy Burrard Inlet. They'd been studying Robert Kroetsch's long poem "The Ledger" for several weeks now. An aunt in Edmonton had given the poet a ledger of a watermill in Ontario, kept by her father. His ancestors were too engrossed in work to imagine their lives as history, so this was all that was left—columns of money accrued alongside columns of money spent.

"You can imagine it," Eira said, knocking her Docs against

the roof, passing Matthew the blunt—a book softened with time spent in a dry wood drawer, a rough hand, the enduring pale trace of blue ink like the blood of a relative never met. The intent is lost; all that's left is the particularity of this dead man's zero, how and where it meets itself. The space between the columns of accounts is vast and full of possibility. A darkness to stand in. Eira's hands made sweeping circles in the air as she went on. Matthew imagined strands of purple yarn stemming from her fingertips, attaching to these columns on the other end, like some kind of loom. Thinking this way was strange to him and he cleared his throat. Eira saw him nodding to what she was saying. Despite the fact that all the other second-years in the class wanted a "message," Matthew seemed to understand, as she did, that you could return to a poem again and again, for its ongoing mystery.

Once it was too late to make it back to class, they would head for the pub in the cellar of the Students' Union Building. This was before it had been renovated to resemble a sports bar, crowned with TV sets, harshly-lit beer ads for pool table lamps. Back then, in the early '90s, the furniture was left over from the '70s, grubby with a well-worn radicalism. It created a dim excitement around them. You would get a sandwich with a big piece of leaf lettuce hanging out, made by a German exchange student smiling at you in a colourful head wrap. There was semi-political rock music in the background: The Tragically Hip, Pearl Jam, 54-40.

Here, Eira sat across from Matthew for several hours, once a week, for thirteen weeks one fall. Their conversations had been long and involved; though, thinking back, she couldn't remember what they'd talked about. In class, they'd been discussing whether the New American Poetry was good for Canadian writers. Eira thought so. She had learned that how you know, and what you invent, comes from the senses of your own body in geography—how your body breaths and moves in the landscape. As they talked about whatever they talked about, Matthew's face became something living in Eira, always before her. It looked up from under the angled bangs, and exploded in laughter. Cheeks and eyes tilted and polished, a Dutch painting. He was like Holden Caulfield. She'd read that book twelve times by the time she was fifteen, she told him.

Near the end of the fall term, as Eira stood over Matthew with one arm raised, shaking it into her peacoat, he looked up at her like he was one of those sad maidens on shore. As though he understood time better than she did. He said, "If you weren't going to Europe," but Eira, only twenty-two, was. Besides, it had been a year of interesting men, and Matthew was already dating someone. Back then, Eira was toying with the idea of becoming a painter. She had taken a few college classes, and had completed a few portraits, all of ex-lovers. She would keep the detail of Matthew's Dutch eye, like a tilted almond, in mind. All of her paintings began this way, with some unusual gesture, some detail of the face that she recalled. When something ended, Eira returned to the detail and began the portrait. The more she worked it out, the more the real person didn't matter anymore. Facing the work, one didn't mind losing the person. She had already finished several of these, successfully, and now conceived of portraits not as a way to remember, but as a way to be rid of someone. She had found the trick to get past the pain of love.

Shortly after she arrived in Norway, a postcard came with a God's-eye view of their university on it. On the other side, Matthew had written that he had gotten engaged. That's funny, Eira thought, holding the postcard for a moment before returning to whatever she was doing, kilometres away in the well-designed Scandinavian dorm room. She had not imagined him following her, or waiting, chaste, for her return.

When Eira got home from her student exchange a year later, it was the month Matthew was set to be married; she found out the night she arrived, during one of her roommate's parties. Matthew was there; he and her roommate had grown up together in a suburban community. Through her bedroom wall, while unpacking, she heard him mention the date; then they began to banter with fondness about their bored youth. She could hear Matthew imitating the professor on *Gilligan's Island* who could make anything from anything. "Oh look, duct tape and a coconut. Let's make a bomb!" Matthew exploded with laughter. Eira's roommate sometimes told her stories about Matthew, how he'd always had this eccentric part to him; once in high school, during a federal election, he had run around the neighbourhood in the middle of the night, uprooting whatever Green Party signs he could find, replanting them across his staunchly Conservative neighbour's yard. Eira had laughed out loud; somehow, in her head, the signs had transformed into bowing pink flamingos burning golden azure in the calculated light of suburban walkway lanterns.

Matthew left the busy party without saying goodbye. Eira ran downhill and found him at the bus stop. Together, they sat on the dusty East Van curb and whatever it was Matthew was saying with his sweeping hands, his long, straight fingers that were squared off at the ends, he sounded sure of the life he was about to build. Of the marriage to Stephanie, of the house he was going to buy in the suburb he grew up in. And she had met someone too, while she was away. Someone with blue eyes that continued to shock her, who had left his country and crossed an ocean to be with her, to her surprise. This, then, was the real beginning of their lives. It was the last time they would see each other before they were both married.

Over the next few years, every once in a while, Eira and Matthew would find a reason to get together for coffee. A mutual friend was in town. For a few hours, they would sit facing each other across a table, the way they did when they first met. Afterwards, Eira would walk around downtown and lay down on some park grass to calm down. A week or so would go by, and the feeling, and the questions that she felt were mostly moral, would go away. Five years passed like this; then Matthew had a child. That's funny, Eira thought. She found out from a mutual friend in Edmonton, where she'd moved to go to grad school. Not long after, he wrote her an email saying he would be coming there on business, and could they meet? He had secured a contract to organize her city's utilities through digital archiving: her water, her electricity.

On the coast, Eira had taken quite a while with her BA. She'd only finished because her father had suggested he would like to come to the ceremony. And now she was doing her Master's in Alberta. She had known the city she was moving to was colourless, a gigantic cold darkness most of the year, but when her husband left her, after he'd found a letter she'd never sent, she felt it was right to go somewhere with few distractions. Where she could be forgotten. She had a picture of herself in a nice little apartment, bent over a desk, snow blowing about through the blackness beside her, outside the window. She would read and write all the time, as a kind of light; "live a life of the mind," as her father said. Then she would return.

But it hadn't been going this way. Nothing grew most of the year. Few people bothered with their garden beds, or the planter boxes outside their storefronts. Eira had not anticipated missing things like flowers, greenery, the edge of the water so much. She felt claustrophobic picturing herself in the middle of all that land. But she'd heard Prairie People feel the same way looking out at the Pacific.

Time seemed to spread around her the same way. She got her first glimpse of Prairie-time on her drive in to Edmonton. She pulled over beside a little wood Métis house collapsing along the side of the highway. Later, she would be told there are many of these standing, still. A patience or tolerance afforded by Prairie sprawl. She stood inside the exposed room that was missing its roof like a stage set and looked at the hundred-year-old moment of departure. Fixed by the weather, several generations had been flattened into a thin stratum: part of a curtain, now wallpaper; bits of a child's pajamas and lace blended into a newspaper, illegible; a cleaning cloth petrified against a kitchen chair.

Shortly after settling in, Eira found out the city was nicknamed "Deadmonton." A man next to her in the rundown Safeway checkout overheard her old area code and interrogated her; why would anyone leave Lotusland? he sneered. She'd never heard her city called that before. She walked down Edmonton streets and boys, bored since they were born, whizzed Slurpees at her head from speeding trucks. She joked with other students that it must be a ritual she didn't understand, not being from here. She took up jogging because people said you had to do something physical when you were at grad school or you'd gain fifty pounds or kill yourself. It was the reason the university had manufactured a holiday in the winter, Reading Week, and had sealed all the windows around campus—too many students were jumping out of towers. People always talked about the wide prairie sky as a saving grace, but this sky had nothing to do with Eira. "Yeah, you better run!" the boys yelled, crashing by, decorative frozen brass balls jangling from their trailer hitches. What did the big sky matter, Eira wondered, with all this dirt? That was the other name for here. Dirt City. Sometimes when she drove around, Eira passed large brown patches of ground that had been spray-painted green. She was told this was done when the city was using aerial photography to promote its green spaces. Still, from even further up, from space, you could see the black of the Tar Sands. Whatever came up from that black swamp was in the air, had accumulated in yellow dust on her window sill, turned her shiny jewelry a molten grey. More reason to stay inside. This was the kind of city people came to for a few years and never left, but not like Paris.

Eira had only come for a two-year degree, and was going to leave one day. She had been bitten by love, but she wasn't planning to stay in this darkness forever. Everyone told her she would not make money as a painter, so at some point she'd decided to be realistic and become a teacher. Another art history student laughed when she found out Eira had come here to study the Flemish master Jan van Eyck. Why? Eira asked. Because, she pointed out, Van Eyck's inspiration came from the beauty of his immediate world. He was surrounded by thick folding fabrics, rich fruits and fat dead birds falling off tables, lacy architecture. Eira laughed, too. The prairie town was known for its natural light, but she couldn't stand to look at what it fell on— taupe slabs of modernism, lines as straight as a farmer's mouth.

They were dismantling an old theatre in the heart of downtown to put up a "temporary" parking lot that would serve a newly erected business tower for the hydro company—its steps were lined with blue neon like a Vegas casino. But the Art History department wasn't helping, either. Each succeeding batch of first-years was instructed to bang together pieces of rusted scrap metal into large-scale, abstract, '60s-esque sculptures that were then unloaded all over the city, like old cars on front lawns... they *were* old cars on lawns. How embarrassing, Eira thought. Like continuing to insist a toilet is art—beyond the first moment of surprise, the sudden turn in history that made it so. The few attractive nineteenth-century buildings left in the city had become slums, neglected by greedy landlords waiting for another boom until their floors and rafters were littered with dead and dying birds. Or they had been burned to the ground in unlikely fires. Still, in her room with her books, Eira could withstand all this for a while. At least, she thought, *I have the flowers of myself.* The line from the poem repeated itself as she sat by the black window, looking through the old master's portraits.

Through the long winters, Eira began to spend mornings in front of the TV. The light, the colour, and the noise were comforting. Once in a while, she would get a letter from her retired father on the coast, teasing her that he saw a crocus that morning, poking up through the snow. If she made it to her desk to see what had been written the day before, it rang false, as though each day were pulling her from sleep to weave together a blanket of other people's voices. She hated writing about art, as it turned out. Things like applying for car insurance, making arrangements at the bank, writing to a distant relative, began to seem like enormous tasks belonging to a kind of life she was far away from.

So when Matthew's email arrived with the subject line "Flash From the Past," she felt an unexpected excitement run through her body; it had come out of what she thought was a final silence. Despite its casual tone, the business he had to do in Edmonton, Eira felt it was the promise of return. She put her cheek against the keyboard; its warmth soaked into her.

Along with this email, Matthew sent Eira a link to a family website he had created as part of a research project he was working on—to develop technologies that connect institutional and personal archives in a worldwide database. The aim was to enhance collective memory, he said. He had done a master's in archival studies and become a digital archivist.

"There is a Romanticism around archivism," he said in his email, "searching in the old, dark caves of overgrown libraries." But he had decided to be realistic and get into the private sector, join the IT people. Most people's eyes glaze over when he begins talking about his work, but basically what he does is try to manage memory through open system software: make otherwise obsolescent documents immediate, transparent, accessible forever.

"Preservation," he said, "is the backbone of all human society." Eira imagined his information as veins of light shooting out and illuminating the whole world at once.

"You could constantly update your old files to new formats, or save your old clunky computers... but that would be a recipe for insanity, wouldn't it?" he laughed.

Eira pictured a Charlemagne scribe in his Dark Age, contemplating the illuminated manuscript he would spend a lifetime on, as though it were a living thing, a treasure.

"Yes," she wrote back to him, "it would require an unimaginable level of patience with the material world."

She didn't tell him she didn't know how to download music and still used a Discman which meant she could actually tell people the name of the song she was listening to; that she didn't have a cell phone, and still used phone booths, when she could find them, because what would happen to movies if the hero couldn't rush into a phone booth, with rain streaming down the outside of it, to tell his lover he'd made a mistake?

With a touch, Eira brought up the previous ten years of Matthew's archived life. Innumerable compartments of holidays and familial milestones: stages of dress, weight, long hair, then short, beard/no beard, a baby is suddenly two years old. "Our Mexican Holiday," with parallel lawn chairs and drinks raised towards the camera, morphs into "Christmas Dinner," with two families tightly arranged around an oblong table—an oval of faces turned towards her. It created a frenzy in Eira that she'd experienced once before.

She hadn't been given a formal religious upbringing, but as a little girl, Eira had walked past hundreds of paintings in Europe that showed what would happen to you in Hell: people stretched out on racks; spikes running up the centre of them; on the ends of pitchforks, getting tossed into cauldrons. Some of them even in religious outfits! But the paintings themselves, with their carefully preserved, but nevertheless wrinkled and cracked surfaces, were so clearly dated. And there seemed to be a tiered moral and temporal order to things that suggested she didn't need to worry too much. She felt at ease, studying each element of torture carefully.

Then, in Spain, she found herself in front of a painting called *The Millennium Triptych.* Her eyes moved around all the things happening in it: a naked human disappearing into the hairy beak of a birdman; a tree creature farting into the face of a naked woman held down by another tree creature; a musical band of animal demons who had rammed a whistle up the ass of man baring a long horn on his back like a cross. A young man stands, a silhouette in the doorway of a burning windmill. Eira didn't know how to look anymore. Except away. She steadied herself and moved quickly down the bare white tunnel of the gallery.

Later on at university, she came across something about this feeling she'd had, in an essay by John Berger. Though the images are haunting and grotesque, he says, Hell is mostly a matter of space.... *There is no horizon there. There is no continuity between actions, there are no pauses, no paths, no pattern, no past and no future. There is only the clamour of the disparate, fragmentary present.... nowhere is there any outcome. Nothing flows through: everything interrupts. There is a kind of spatial delirium.* He said Bosch's painting was a strange prophesy of the globalized mind, the new economic order.

This delirium was what Eira felt, sitting in front of Matthew's photos. Though they were organized in files by year and occasion, she had pulled them up so quickly it seemed they didn't cover any time at all, were only troubling contradictions in the present. She herself had no similar documents. There were the faces of her portraits, but they were kept under the stairs, or in a storage locker in the last city she lived in. No one looked at those. When, on occasion, she pulled one out, the face had become something unrecognizable, or something other people would categorize as Primitive. Whatever force or understanding was behind the making of it was gone now, could only involve an educated guess. Her paintings were like the Fayum portraits—neither their painters nor their sitters thought about posterity or being remembered. The masks were passports for the underworld, secured a place in eternity. It occurred to Eira then that she had simply been waiting these ten years. But there had been no years. Only an eternal present. If there were a picture of the real expression of her life, of love, Eira thought, it lay in the dark. There was one photo—pretending to want a group shot,

Eira had taken a picture of Matthew in the pub on the last day of class, all those years ago; in it, he is blurred, turning away from the camera.

As it got closer and closer to the date Matthew was to arrive in Edmonton, Eira got more and more productive with her thesis work. She felt lighter, simpler, as though for the first time she could sense what it was like to be one of those people who can envision a future. Someone passed her in the dreary hallway of the Art department and told her she looked like someone in love. Eira was only looking forward to sitting across the table from Matthew again, seeing again the face that was always in front of her. She felt as though she had not had a conversation in years.

The day before Matthew was to arrive, Eira received an email in which he lamented that although he wished he could see her, unfortunately, on close examination, if he were to be honest with himself, he would have to admit that he was in love with her and had been for the many years they had known each other, and that because of everything he had built with his family, they could never see each other again. Eira froze in the grad student lounge. It was the first time he had used the word "love," and he had calmly unfolded the map of his marriage over it, smoothed it down. It was the first real bit of darkness to fall.

Eira needed to get away for a while, to finish her thesis. The northern prairie town seemed not to be isolating enough. When the opportunity came up to housesit a studio home on Protection Island, a small island off the west coast, Eira took it.

The couple who lived there were close family friends, and their house was organized for-contemplation. Every time you visited, there was the old metal milk jug to rest your coffee on, the spare furniture, soft chairs in subtle colours that were angled towards the sea. Simple cast iron pans hung above the stove. Eira had always admired their ability to enjoy life. This winter, they were travelling through Europe, visiting a count in Abruzzi who owned a vineyard. They would return with wine and stories and new recipes involving Italian sausage.

Eira would work all morning. In the afternoon, she would walk around the island that was mapped with names like Pirate's Lane and Treasure Cove. She passed the old wood firehouse, sometimes stumbled across the mucky, hidden duck pond, and made her way down to the sea; her patience and calmness came again when she looked out across the distance to be covered. She was surprised that the ceaseless waves brought nothing back to shore with them. As an afterthought, in the receding afternoon, they left one thing—on a stretch of flat rock, three enormous gaping shells, their backs fused together with barnacles. It looked like an eccentric centrepiece. Eira imagined Matthew and Stephanie's smooth granite countertop, which needed something. She thought of placing this monstrosity on top.

During the night, the slim trunks of the forty-foot firs creaked hard in the wind outside Eira's bedroom window. Afraid of one crashing in, she got up, went to the kitchen, sat at the dark table and opened Matthew's archives. Though she would never see him in the places in the pictures, Eira now knew he had a brown living-room couch. She knew the pattern (the tiny sprays of flowers) on the quaint, country-style bedspread, the one he sleeps under with his wife. And that the art, what passed as art, was hung too high on walls that were left the colourless palette sellers use so buyers can image themselves there, or rather, no one else there before them. In fact, "The New House" was so thoroughly documented that Eira got to know every corner of every room, every part of its yard, front and back—the neighbouring houses, the neighbours. Eira never saw Matthew with his shirt off until "Vacation in Cancun 2002." Though she hadn't noticed it in their weeks together, years ago, there was a sharp thinness to his lower right shin that made his pant leg take an unrealistic, almost comical bend, made one wonder if there was a leg there at all. She learned the minutiae of his family's everyday lives and routines: the name of their local pizza place; that they went on a family vacation the first week of every July; that Simon, his son, loved trains and had the same robin's-egg blue rain-suit Matthew had had as a boy. How strange it was to know these details of his life. She became familiar with all the members of his Dutch family whom she had never met. They smiled out at her every year at Easter and Christmas time.

Over the weeks, Eira's attention was drawn to some extended relative named Billy. He first appeared on "Moving Day," his black hair springing out in parts, dressed in wrinkled army pants and a leather jacket with WARSAW painted in white on the back. The others in the album had on the uniform of-the-day: the slacks and simple sweaters of department store catalogues and government documents. Billy stood out. Eira clicked through "Moving Day," which ended in a party. She studied the expressions, the poses. These revealed only a relaxed boredom, a resigned focus on some exemplary baby playing with a plastic toy on the carpet of the living room in the finished house. Billy was not looking there, but to the edge of the photo; and there was a slight stiffness to his body, as though it were braced against something not visible.

Why had Matthew sent her his family archives? Eira wondered. What could be made of all these portraits? What did he want her to find? It was though she needed a code. She clicked back to "At the Fair," "At the Aquarium," "At the Beach." Perhaps there would be some flaw, some betraying detail—an object in the background acting as a symbol, a small tear in the surface, a spot of discolouration, a scratch that reveals another painting beneath. But they were all the same, digital, but not spontaneous: the family arranged on some old-fashioned trolley car, on park grass amongst windblown leaves, a team in matching shirts. Mother to the left, Father to the right. The baby in the middle will not comply, is busy with something moving in the grass.

After several weeks of scanning, Eira abandoned the family portraits, their even-tempered faces and careful arrangement in front of some opulent gardenia bush. She searched the island home and found a TV in a closet. With a hanger turned into an antenna, and if she pressed the thing against the north window, she got two channels. One aired outlines of fiery Italian soap opera stars fighting and making love behind a wall of black-and-white fuzz. The clearer channel aired mostly commercials. Four or five times a night, a housewife with tight curls like Stephanie's turned smugly to the audience and said, "There are things going on in your house that you may not know about," then she sprayed down her sofa with a fine mist of chemicals. Eira wondered what viewer bought the idea that a shot of fake flowers erases anything. The product claimed to attack at the source—the smelly dog? the pungent husband? The housewife covered all the surfaces; she pulled apart curtains and turned over pillows.

Over the next few weeks, Eira got to know the commercial channel well. While she washed the dishes in the afternoon with the detergent it insisted on, she watched a woman dragging her husband by his heels down a hallway to bed, four or five times a day. The theme was back pain. When the man's legs passed by for the hundredth time, Eira finally noticed the occasional table behind him—its carefully placed, nondescript white vase on top. It was no place, but it was oddly familiar. Eira tossed the cloth, went to the family archives and began opening files. The hallway in the commercial was almost identical to the hallway in "The New House." She had thought, for the sake of the archive, the stray bits of daily life had been thrown down the basement stairs, been hidden behind doors. But now the gallery of "The New House" seemed like a montage of household products: his living room, a vacuum commercial post-stain; his bedroom, an aspirin commercial, or a bad cough; his kitchen, something about a fast-cooking side dish. Like a commercial, Eira realized, Matthew's family photos invited you into intimate parts of a home and then presented you with nothing of life. *Spatial Delirium*, shallow and wide. Space itself was what Billy was braced against. Not devils with pitchforks, but a beige showroom and an acute awareness of being forever in it; his stiffness marked a premonition particular to the doomed. *My hell is no worse than yours,* Eira thought, caught inside the glowing rectangle at the dark island table. No worse than that Platonic white chair-and-a-half. That bland mirror echoing the empty wall. That floor lamp, lost, and over-illuminating the empty corner.

Were Matthew's family photos that different from those on his business site? Eira clicked. Here Matthew faced the camera with calmness. It was the perfect face for business, she thought: a floating, pale disc, smoother and wider than Matthew's real face, spreading out to meld with the backside of the computer screen. It reminded Eira of Egyptian art, which she never enjoyed. She could admire its sleekness, but became easily bored by the stubborn refusal to appear three-dimensional; the endless tiny hieroglyphs reminded her of computer code—something mathematical, some abstract way of thinking about themselves. On his homepage, Matthew sat cross-legged on a royal purple couch ornately framed with gold. It was a silly photo. He looked like a king. Not just because of the seat. Eira had read in a book on the history of portraiture that a full frontal pose was often used to make a king out of an ordinary man: it was a pose that asked for nothing from the viewer; it stated an ideal. The business photo was no different than how Matthew arranged his family. Eira clicked back. They, too, were marked by the rigid frontality, as though they had stopped whatever they were doing to accommodate the lens. All the eyes of the photographs stared out as if to say, "You can stop your searching. There's nothing more to find here, this is everything there is."

Dutch seventeenth-century portraits of married couples are rarely joyous in expression, but their customary reticence was frequently mitigated by the artificially casual disposition of their figures in a comfortable domestic environment.

Eira stared at the six eyes. Then she started layering album upon album, over them, exploding photo upon photo, until she arrived at a file called "Miscellaneous." In it was a picture of Matthew walking alone in a blue suit. At a conference or a wedding, there was not enough background to tell. He was rushing forward, looking back over his shoulder. A ray of light had landed on his turned cheekbone and exposed lines around the almond eye. The neck of the blue suit was not lying smooth against the white collar; the turn of his head had pulled it away and left a long, dark opening, like a fault line. It seemed to call the suit a lie. This was the flaw. The photograph she was meant to find, she thought. The sunlight caught in Matthew's eye began churning. Whirling, it seemed, like Van Gogh's *Starry Night*, towards darkness, his iris, where it burst outwards with great speed and caught Eira across the face. She felt sick for a moment, closed her eyes, the narrow opening widened beneath her, she fell forward into darkness. When she came to, she was standing with her head against the glass, her reflection leaning into her.

It can take people so long to figure out what, in hindsight, seems to be the simplest thing. It had taken Eira months to notice this photo of Matthew, caught in a turn. It had taken humans ages to allow themselves to be painted as they are. One random day in the fourteenth century, an artist figured out how to turn a religious icon into a human being. With shadowing and a bit of perspective, he rounded out the edges of its body— as though with a kind of pity. When she was a child, Eira liked Giotto's paintings because at least one person in them—cloaked, hunched over, usually looking a bit worried—was turned towards her, where she stood looking at them. Later, she would read that this was the very thing that Giotto was remembered for. With it, he had led artists out of the Dark Ages and lit the way for the Renaissance.

Another year passed before Matthew came back to Edmonton, where Eira was still living. She had returned from the island with a rough draft of her first chapter, and had finished the bloody thing off six months later. She hadn't planned on staying on in Edmonton after her degree, but she didn't have a reason to leave. Matthew's contact was sudden, unexpected, like before: another email out of the silence to say he was coming, this time for a final review of the project he'd started several years ago, and they really should meet now.

What did the women of history do as they waited onshore, from their widow's walks, their towers? They wove, they grew their hair, they pulled the image apart with shaky fingers. They did not look at the world directly. They wove it together again tight, tight, tight, refusing any other possibility. What did the picture look like? Woven together and taken apart so many times, threadbare before it was completed. The whole thing eventually tossed aside at the first sight of a return, of real arms to entwine, to be entangled in.

Matthew arrived between snowfalls. The sidewalks were clear. The snow had been pushed to the side and what was left had compacted into boulders of darkly translucent ice, "Like yellow topaz jewels," he thought on the way to Eira's address. Her apartment block looked grey and run-down, but then so did most of the buildings in the city, he'd noticed. He rang the buzzer and heard her voice in jolts through the intercom. Buzzed in, he entered the stairwell, descended beneath a dim, chipped gold chandelier, passed a landing of dirty-white and leafy wallpaper, an old washing machine against a wall, descended another set of stairs. Stood in her doorframe.

. . .

. . .

. . .

Three days later Eira received an email:

...] was in a fog. Drifting through his workday, suspended between two lives, unable to touch down in either one. Could they [let go?] He was having trouble letting go. The idea of her had opened something in him. She would always [...] He would never [forget her].

Several months later, she received another email.

He was doing well since they were last in touch. He had had some good discussions with Stephanie that had really turned things around—though it was to her, not Stephanie, that he had told the story of how he left work that day, drove through the rain to the bird sanctuary, climbed the old gun tower on the edge of the marshland, stared out across the grey sky and water to nothing and realized he was alone in the world; but this was something he was working on. He had begun looking online into some courses on marriage counseling.

Ironically, she had once again made it possible for him to return to his life with a new kind of vigour, certitude, as though she were the marker that helped him understand his various milestones. How was it that she had always stuck out from his life like a sore thumb, a piece of the puzzle that didn't fit? Why did life always offer you more than you needed? And yet, he had always returned to her. It was as if his imaginary life with her ran parallel to his real one. However, he was afraid he could not be as certain as she was of their love. He had never suggested that he would leave Stephanie; he could not stand the idea of not being able to see his son every day. Besides, he had never been sure how much of what she'd stirred in him had been because of the drinking he was doing back then. Ultimately, it may have been a garden-variety romance he'd felt for her. His drinking was something Stephanie understood. The point was, there should be no sense of false hope between them; any further meeting would just result in another round of forever unanswerable questions, searching.

In the meanwhile, life continued at full throttle. He was extremely busy at work, at home with renos, with Stephanie and Simon, and also training for the Sun Run, which was nice. He was getting ready to go to Japan in a few weeks and looking forward to it, as long as he could deliver the work that everyone was expecting to be completed. Speaking of which, he had to get back to work.

He hoped that she was getting on with life and that her schooling and painting were going well. He wished her serenity and happiness.

Several weeks later, the online family archive activity seemed to stop. Perhaps Matthew's project was complete, or he had lost interest in it. At any rate, if he'd continued, Eira no longer had access to it. The last album she could open contained eighteen photos, and was titled "Billy and Lindsay's Wedding."

So, things had turned out all right for Billy, after all. Amongst the photos there was one of Matthew's family. Stephanie was holding a new baby, a girl named Phoebe. Eira wondered if Matthew recalled that this was the name of Holden Caulfield's sister. Simon, now a young boy, was next to her. Matthew, standing behind them all, had one arm around Stephanie, and the other around his young son. The baby was stretched out and unconsciously resting her hand on her brother's shoulder. Eira noticed that, with the head lolling back and arm that way, she looked like one of Parmigianino's disproportionately long, adult-looking baby Jesuses. They were all facing forward for the picture, of course, and so could not see that they had formed a ring.

Eira spent the days looking at the photo of the blue suit. Matthew caught in a turn, rushing off somewhere. She looked at all the other photos, the faces that made no appeal. His face that made no appeal until she could see in it a face she'd looked at many times. She pulled down a giant art book and leafed through to a self-portrait of Jan van Eyck. Beneath it, the art historian says:

This face, like all of Jan's portraits, remains a psychological puzzle. It might be described as "even-tempered" in the most exact sense of the term, its character traits balanced against each other so perfectly that none can assert itself at the expense of the rest. As Jan was fully capable of expressing emotion (we need only to recall the faces of the crowd in The Crucifixion)

the stoic calm of his portraits surely reflects his conscious ideal
of human character rather than indifference or lack of insight.

There was a caption in the gilt frame. "As I Can." Eira pulled out her computer. It turned out to be the first half of the Flemish proverb, "As I can, but not as I would." This mysterious saying appears in at least three of Van Eyck's paintings. One of them a marriage portrait. Had he meant the limit of his materials? His time? Something else? Perhaps it wasn't the photo of the turn she was supposed to find, Eira thought. Maybe it was the nearly indiscernible, mysterious strain about the eyes of all the rest, looking to her. The historian says:

The slight strain about the eyes seems to come from gazing into a mirror.

On the couch, Eira lay with the art history textbook heavy on her stomach, running one hand back and forth along the carpet. Idly, she turned a page and there was *The Millennium Triptych*. The reproduction was, of course, much smaller and less detailed that the original in Spain, and so less disturbing. It was clear, the art historian spoke again, that Bosch didn't believe in purgatory. People didn't have to wait for happiness, just as they didn't have to wait for Hell. It could be had on Earth. In his Garden, people were plants and animals were people, dancing, resting, loving. But, Eira thought, time had shown that humans and the natural world hadn't returned to each other in this way at all, had they? All of the world's frozen secrets were being forced out in her lifetime. Across the North, a glut of woolly mammoths had appeared from what was once deep ice; exposed and wet on their sides, they were born again, unasking. The voice on the radio said: "Good news, the tusks could put an end to the illegal elephant-ivory trade!" Meanwhile, a thousand doves had fallen out of the sky in Rome, the same thing had happened with blackbirds in Arkansas. Some experts claimed it was the bang of fireworks. Some still insisted it was a mystery.

Eira wondered if Matthew had thought that all his photos would add up to something. As though she could make it so—as though she could pull out something iconic just by looking and looking, the way a masterpiece was forever full of searching— both viewer and painter, over the years, looking again and again at the same cherished thing. Like Van Gogh's haystack or Cezanne's hillside. For the first time, Eira considered how she appeared to Matthew, inside the internet. A smattering of conference papers, a few publications, mention in an art review from several years ago. No images—just darkness, as she sat fixed in front of the screen, waiting for him to finish.

The art book is beside her on the floor. It has gotten dark outside and Eira's eyes are closed and she is hardly breathing. It's the carbon dioxide in people's breath that is destroying the earliest images in the world, says the host of the documentary— paintings that had, until recently, been preserved, hidden deep in caves. Eira had turned on the television several hours ago and it is now half asleep in the glow of the British series *How Art Made the World*.

The Cave of Altamara, Spain: Around 13,000 years ago, a rockfall sealed the entrance of the cave. In the late nineteenth century, a tree fell and cleared the rocks. A nine-year-old girl named Maria found the opening, held a lantern up to the animals on the ceiling and called to her father. The father fell ill and died trying to convince the world these paintings were not a hoax. They couldn't be real, the prehistoric scholars said, they were too advanced, too fine. When Picasso saw them, he remarked: "We have learned nothing."

Soon after, all over the world, similar cave painting were found and questions were asked. Why would people make paintings in the deep rock where they couldn't be seen? Why pictures of animals they didn't hunt? And most importantly, what were the abstract dots and lines that ran across them? There have been many theories along the way, the host continued, each one corresponding to the Idea of its Age. To Eira, the painted dots and lines looked like the ellipses and brackets used when salvaging Ancient Greek poems: to denote guessed-at words, their order and modifications, sometimes entire missing fragments—important parts of the story that will remain lost. The middles or ends of Sappho's love poems, for instance.

...] It's no use
Mother dear, I
Can't finish my
Weaving

You may

Blame Aphrodite

soft as she is

she has almost

killed me with

love for that boy [...

Her poetry was written on papyrus scrolls, durable paper made from the stalks of water plants. These scrolls had been torn into strips and used to form the cartonnage that lined mummy coffins. They were poems saved only because they were done with, buried with the dead, like portraits never to be shown. Some scroll strips were found on rubbish heaps, others pulled, in wadded-up lumps, from the mouths of mummified crocodiles.

Our current Age claims the dots and lines running across the cave art replicate the flashes the brain makes up in total darkness, in a trance—that the first images came not from nature, but from the brain's hardwiring. Amongst the South African rock paintings, there is a famous one of an eland, head down, hairs on end, ankles crossed, stumbling towards death. The shaman—cloven-hoofed, hairs on end—holds the eland's tail and is also crossed at the ankles. Eira is not surprised to hear that what the head in the dark is most interested in is its own workings, in seeing itself... and that the entranced mind that has seen itself moves towards death. The missing part.

How was this shaman-artist like Matthew who had, when walking with Eira along Vancouver's Seawall many years ago, talked about himself as a visionary? Shamans journeyed through the sea to the underworld so they could come back to heal people. Now, in Eira's lifetime, everything below the ocean's surface will be a dead zone, devoid of breath—all because of Matthew's golden wires of promise—communication's entrails dragging along the bottom of the ocean from here to the old world, through nothing but sludge and the occasional jellyfish.

The internet is not the sea. The line repeats itself. Eira is almost asleep now, so still she could be a photograph. She is barely aware of the traffic outside on 109th Street turning into rolling waves. She wonders if she'll ever return to the coast. Back when men still travelled in ships, Baudelaire had asked the question: why was the sight of the sea so infinitely and eternally attractive? and had answered it: because the sea gives the ideas of immensity and movement at once.

Afterword

Once in a while, over the years, Matthew would send a line about his research projects into the viral virtual world. "What would you do if, say, you had something valuable like a song or a love letter on an old 5¼-inch floppy? How would you read it?" One could argue that his references to art and such were a way of professing his undying love for Eira—a lamenting head cut off from a body that had never touched her.–Otherwise,

Matthew continued to drift easily downstream, his life with Stephanie and his three children moved ever forward towards the future. Sources suggest he became very well known in his field, designing digital methods to preserve the flaking and problematic materials of history. Bathed in unifying screen light, he flew around the world asking the question, "How can we enlighten the people with open source software? In an ideal world, the code would be available to everyone. All knowledge will be available, fixed, present always. Nothing will be lost," said the floating head. The people sang its praises.

In some versions of the story, Matthew is eventually torn apart by numerous secret affairs; in others, whatever it was that drew him to Eira eventually ate away at him, though this went undetected by those around him. Another version claims he became very religious. It is unclear whether Eira ever moved back to the coast, and there is no material evidence that she ever finished Matthew's portrait. If she continued to make art, she never posted it on the internet. Eventually, Eira ceased doing anything that made her visible online, which means all connection to her is now lost. And so we know nothing more about her.

TO THE DOGS

It is a feeling of relief, almost of pleasure, at knowing yourself at last genuinely down and out. You have talked so often of going to the dogs—and well, here are the dogs, and you have reached them, and you can stand it.

— George Orwell, *Down and Out in Paris and London*

Part I

Someone take these dreams away,
That point me to another day

— **Joy Division,** *"Dead Souls"*

I have always thought that as long as you can't imagine your life as a great work of literature you are probably doing all right in the world. In other words, you must be holding it together OK, to yourself, and aren't flawed in some horrible way that makes you fascinating and dismissible at once. "Thank goodness that's not me," the reader thinks, closing the old tragedy with a thud and shaking her head on the way to the fridge for a bottle of fizzy Italian water. I, however, see people this way all the time, everywhere I go. For example, there is the waitress at The

Ordinary, my morning coffee spot, who is too beautiful to be a waitress in the unsophisticated, ugly city we both live in. And this alone has changed her whole personality, has made her mean.

I suspect that, secretly, most people imagine they have a mortal flaw. They're just unable to put words to it. Still, they've always sensed it, been circling it, maybe for years. Maybe seen it recognized, flash back from the eyes of a near stranger. Then, one day, because of something they didn't mean to do, there it is, clear and simple, their flaw. And there they are, not like a tragic king, but like everyone else—and the camera of their life zooms out until they're walking around in a sea of ordinary people.

My name is Riel. After Louis Riel. My father was a professor and an amateur historian who loved revolutionary figures that stood up for the underdog. The disenfranchised and the trampled-on. Big boots to fill. If I could imagine myself as a hero in the kind of film I like, I wouldn't have a name. Clint Eastwood never has a name in his westerns. "High Plains Drifter" doesn't count as a name. Uma Thurman doesn't have a name in *Kill Bill.* She is simply "The Bride." Or I forget their names. When you are a benevolent killer passing through town, your name is beside the point.

I was a bride once. I knew when it was over that this man had been my undoing. But it wasn't much of an undoing, more the kind that's like you're watching a movie: you can never really get inside of it. As seriously as you take it, you still have a comic raised eyebrow about the whole thing. I suppose in part I never wanted to put myself in the position where I could be ruined by love. But I knew after it was all over that this man was probably going to be the love of my life, and that I wouldn't love again, for any amount of time anyway. I wished then that I had chosen something I couldn't have the inside-raised-eyebrow about. That I hadn't felt too guilty to go with the one who could have taken my heart for good—the one with the wife and kids—since I was going to live the rest of my life alone, anyway. At this point, anything else seems exhausting, or redundant. It is, in the end, staying with the wrong person for too long that really does you in. So far I'm right about that.

But there was one other since then. Billy. And I think it was only because he could see my past on me, right from the start. He had a nose for the chronically lonely. He was lonely himself. When I met Billy, I was serving at a bar called The Blackhoof. It was the kind that people like, with old brass and substantial wood. I was sitting at the end of the bar when Billy crossed the room to tell me I looked like someone who had not been loved. But... I had been. Plenty of times. And I was one of those few kids who knew for sure that their parents didn't hate them. It rattled me all the same, because who says things like this if they're not in a movie? Normally, I never have trouble sitting alone. If that happens, I just imagine myself as a woman with a big secret who's running from the law. But his coarseness threw me. Billy was clearly a con man. Not that that has ever stopped a woman from getting involved. No, what got to me was that whatever Billy was, he really *was* like a character in a movie; but unlike me, he had obviously never imagined himself this way.

Billy was tall, and the thinnest man I'd ever been attracted to. When he walked fast with his hands in his pockets, he was like a Giacometti sculpture. Alone in space. Irreducible. From the side, his nose looked kind of smashed in, like a boxer's, but from the front, it was long and elegant. Almost Byzantine. All his features were fine, and he had thin skin and a full mouth. I've always been a sucker for feminine-looking men, maybe because they seem more sensitive, like they might be good to you. When he stood close, looking down into my face, with his long bangs, Billy was like a hero in an Irish film about one of their civil wars. Maybe this was because most of the time, he wore an old faded army jacket and pants. Though, when he took me to a film about Michael Collins, he told me that the early Irish army had no uniforms, and even had to smuggle guns because they were working-class volunteers. He'd like to have been a war hero, I think.

I couldn't tell whether Billy could tell I knew he was conning me, but I could feel that old inside eyebrow being raised, which meant I was game. I knew I had the advantage, that I was smarter than him. And if you're a woman and careful, you can take this a long way, since most men don't let themselves consider this a possibility, really. No one uses the term "con woman." Calculating women are something else. Something that means you have to use your body, too. But what I did, I always just took a step back into myself. I watched, listened with compassion, and said things I sort of meant... but mostly said to settle, put words to, some uncertainty in a man. I suppose you could say that makes me a con artist too. But I didn't think about it that way, then. I suppose because I write stories, I thought it was different. If you write, you will use anything you can if it works. There's a reason you might go into certain dangerous areas with a person, even if you're not writing about them at the time, and just imagine you might somewhere down the road. I don't know why you would go there if not to produce something in the end. I don't know why Billy did.

I'd been working at the bar for nearly two years when Billy came up to me that night to me to tell me about the sadness he could see in me. Since I was a little girl, men have been coming up to me to tell me I look sad, or that I should smile; usually it's just when I'm thinking about something fairly hard. In fact, I'm usually quite happy until they tell me otherwise. As for the other thing, I've found when people tell you they can see something in you, it usually just means they want to take something from you. I knew that, but all the same, I kept wondering if Billy really could see something in me that others couldn't. Why is it that even when people know it, they'll go on letting themselves be conned? Like they're watching a magic show.

One time when I was a kid, I was at a birthday party where the parents had hired this magician. All through his act, I kept guessing how he did the tricks and then explaining them out loud to everyone. I could see him getting angrier and angrier, but I couldn't seem to stop. At the end, he made all the kids balloon animals, except me. But it wasn't really my fault. I thought the whole point was to try to figure out the trick. I think men are the same way with women. You know and they know it's a trick, but you're just supposed to go along with the show, think it's magic, even if you can tell them how it's done. You're not supposed to let everybody know you've figured it out. But I guess they see it in my eyes... that I know, and that's why men usually leave me in the end.

But Billy was beautiful. So this time I went along. Not beautiful in a way everyone would think, though. In fact, most people thought he was ugly. You had to be up close to him to see it. From far away, he looked like a greasy punk. That's what people said to me—people who only knew him to see him, from the bar or around. But you had to be in his aura for a while to catch his beauty, at certain moments. Like one time, Billy and me were standing out back of the bar after closing time, in the parking lot under the bright floodlight in winter. Billy's face would go completely white in a certain hard light, like a Cassavetes film. We'd just smoked a joint and he was smiling and talking about nothing.

"Hey," he says, his whole delicate face laughing, thin crinkles around his eyes and mouth. "What did the leper say to the prostitute?" I was laughing so hard I could barely speak.

"No, no, no. No, don't say it, I don't want to know!"

"You can keep the tip!"

He was laughing and looking at me, eyes blurry with tears, and I think that's when I knew I'd fallen in love with him. It's crazy what I fall in love with. A second later, I thought, hey, tips are what you give a waitress. I was a waitress. Billy was the leper and I was the prostitute. But this insight didn't change anything, at the time. Billy had a way of making you ignore certain things that occurred to you.

I suppose part of the reason I started seeing Billy was that he was the cook at a bar on the corner of the street I worked on. He called himself a chef, but also he painted. There was a hunger about him. One you might associate with artist types. Maybe that's true. I suppose that was what attracted me most. Though... at first I didn't realize that was what it was. I flattered myself that it was genuine desire, desire and nerve, that he would have the gumption to pursue me the way he did. Not many men allow themselves to do that, I thought. And somewhere along the way, some book or movie teaches you that this is evidence of true love.

By the end, I realized Billy was just endlessly hungry, the way a dog is. I'd later compare Billy to various animals. I would tell people: Billy's like a slug—moving nowhere fast but leaving an impressive, gleaming trail of shit behind him. But, as incorrect as it may seem, since Billy was poor and had a hard time early on, really, comparing him to a dog is more of a compliment than it seems. We forgive animals their desire in a way we don't humans. A dog sitting staring at his owner eating ice cream isn't disgusting the way a man in a bar staring at a woman is. A dog waiting outside for his master, not noticing you pat it, isn't pathetic the way a human is, in the same state. An animal isn't self-conscious, so it can't be made ugly by the embarrassment of its want. Billy was like this. He would stare at me for hours at the bar, watching my every turn for a bottle, every pour, moving across the floor with the tray. An animal's focus. He never tried to hide it. His hunger was unapologetic.

It was this direct thing about Billy that people liked. And I guess it came from his hard life. And so people were always forgiving him for the things he did. Before I met him, he had moved down to Michigan for a while, to be with someone he was supposed to marry. When he decided that, instead of marrying, it was time to leave, he jumped on a bus with the girl's money and came back here. The fact that Billy told me this at all, he must have known already that I would forgive him. According to Billy, the girl's father still sounds pleasantly surprised whenever he calls with the latest promise of returning for all his stuff.

The thing is, most people just like the feeling of somebody paying attention. And Billy made you feel this way. Right up until you realized he wasn't. Once, when we were lying in bed, he told me the way I breathe is quick and shallow. That I breathed less than most people. I thought you had to feel a part of someone to notice something like that. Or at least share the same understanding of something. But I guess artists notice all kinds of small things about people and it doesn't mean they love you, *per se*.

I took it that Billy was the only one who noticed I wasn't very brave, and this was a great relief to me. At school, everyone just kept expecting the best of you, even though the rumour was that half the English Department was on anti-depressants. We were all living on top of a lie here, living on top of a patch of oil you could see from space. 50% higher cancer, asthma, MS, and you name it, than anywhere else in the country. This was a place of the right now, at all cost. It meant your family farm would have a snake of oil-pipe running over it, or an electric tower plunked down next to it, that in time would give your five-year-old kid a death rattle. Our government didn't bother contributing to a heritage fund. They'd rather lower taxes. And what for, so people could buy bigger trucks and come into my bar and drink their hundred-dollar bills away on rye and Cokes.

So this is how I breathed. I hadn't noticed. But Billy was very interested in the body and how it dealt with such things. It may have been the one thing he could meet head on. After they discovered the cyst in my breast, Billy used to grab it and squeeze it hard when we were pumping away in the dark. But then, if it comes up in conversation, you find everyone in this town has some kind of chest pain or growth in them, but no one ever leaves, and people still keep throwing their old TV sets into the river that runs through town, where we all have to drink from.

But I suppose you could say Billy's interest was more clinical than courageous. After I left him, the first time, I still heard stories from Billy's kitchen—from our porters who the bartenders sent over for the free meal they got in exchange for serving Billy complimentary pints most of the afternoon, when the kitchen was slow. One time one of our porters, "Boris"—we call him that because he's always going on about how his family is descended from Russian royalty—anyway, Boris ran back with a pizza, all excited, and told us that Billy had lost a tooth. It had started to come loose and he was backed up with orders in the kitchen, so he dug it out with a drinking straw and put it in a glass of Coke and set it on a shelf above the sink to see how long it would take to dissolve. That's what I mean by clinical. When I heard that story, I could forgive Billy a little for everything that had happened, and would happen. Though... I think it's one thing to see how far a body will go, and quite another to see how far a situation will. I mean, it's not like Billy was putting himself in the line of fire, had the courage of battle. As for Billy's attentiveness, his disturbing stare, later on I said Billy was a sociopath, but in fact, I never minded. It turned out to be more believable than any hard evidence of love. Or maybe it was just more interesting.

So I could see all this in Billy right away, and I knew where it came from, too. Billy had two stories he told you: the first was about how he had ridden his bicycle all around Ireland five years ago, and how he was going back one day; and the other was how, at sixteen, he had come home to find his mother dead from an overdose of pain medication. He went with her in the ambulance, anyway. The police questioned his involvement, and later he went to live with his uncle, who was in the military. His father hadn't as of yet decided he was a family man, which he did years later with his second marriage. After his mother died, Billy lived with those kids and his father's wife for a while, until there was a falling-out over some money owed. Billy's father had been in the military also, then was a beatnik for a while, and ended up being a therapist of some kind. He and Billy seldom talked. When they did, it was always about the money, or how Billy should seek professional help. His father said he could refer him to a few good therapists.

There were the stories Billy told me about his life, but also the one I could see and put together the more I got to know him. And when I met Billy, I was sorely in need of a good story. When people from outside of the bar ask where I work, they all say: well, I guess you get some good stories, anyway. As if working in a bar has anything to do with that. When famous writers write their memoirs they often tell you their first job was working as a waitress or something. As soon as they do, though, they're quick to let you know what a horrible waitress they were. I suppose you're supposed to think that their being a horrible waitress means they're really good at writing or something. Like there was nothing else they could be any good at. But I was a good waitress and bartender, and most professionals are surprised to find out that you can make a decent living at it. But it's not a place for interesting stories, just the same old ones. The weekend crowd thinks unexpected things can happen in a bar, that your life could suddenly change. That you could meet someone. But the truth is, nothing ever happens.

Every night when I came in the back door, I'd pass the same regulars along the bar, in some variation, already a few pints in. We had names for most of them. Some of them, like old Nadine, were weird enough that you only had to say their real name with a certain emphasis. Every day, Nadine used to bring our manager, Kent, gifts from IKEA: paper towels, napkins—which were useful, at least—but then a child's mobile, a shower curtain. Kent told her he already had a shower curtain and she told him to use it at the bar, then. When he told her we didn't have a shower at the bar, she got angry and said she wasn't taking it back and he'd just have to find some use for it. One day, she left him some bedsheets, and Kent got pretty pissed and made sure the next day she saw them in the garbage can behind the bar. After that, Old Nadine started staying until 3AM every night and then stumbling out to her car. One time, one of our doorguys found her face-down on the horn, like you would in a movie. After that, she wasn't allowed in anymore, though sometimes people would report her walking around in the alley behind the bar. But Nadine had always tipped, and I had a certain tolerance for her—maybe because she was a woman, and she didn't expect me to smile; and maybe because when she was a kid she supposedly saw her father murder her mother.

The other regulars all had names we gave them: Barstool Bobby, Magic Dave, The Kilt, White Belt Johnny, Squid and Old Rusty, etc. And the time of day they were there, I was the only thing for them to look at. I've got red hair, which I guess is supposed to mean something. They'd try to guess your age, your background. Want to know why you're not married. Do you speak another language. Try to give you a photograph of the kid they're only allowed to see once every two weeks. As if I gave a shit. They've got it all wrong: thinking you're there to share your story, since they all have theirs that they cling to, are itching to tell you—when all your job really is, is to put their pint of beer down in front of them and pry up the sticky coins they leave behind. But they'll keep asking anyway, no matter how busy you keep yourself, finding things to clean at the other end of bar. They've got some romantic idea. Their waitress is the one in folk songs and independent films. She is like some unchanging thing, time standing still, an emblem for failed dreams. If I *did* have one defining story, I wouldn't tell it to them. I came to hate seeing their smiling faces. I'll never write a story about those people.

But I'd been going to grad school and was beginning to get more and more concerned about what all my education was leading to. I suppose I'd learned a lot, and now I owed the bank and the government around forty thousand dollars for it. I kept working at the bar because I could earn more doing that than working as a teacher.

The truth is, I didn't know if I wanted to teach. I remember there was this very funny thing that happened the first year of my program. I had gotten this research assistant job; mainly what I did was look over the professor's articles and make sure the periods were on the right side of the quotation marks, that sort of thing. I'd work in her office, which was in the Old Arts building. It was the only beautiful building on campus. Ivy around the windows. Often, when you were trying to get to and from class, you'd have to work your way around recently graduated brides and their wedding parties who, even though they were business majors, were getting their pictures taken out front. They didn't want to learn in there; they only wanted to stand outside because it was the only half-decent bit of architecture in the city. Gothic-looking, and not just in style. It was crumbling away at the stairs and in other places. You should have seen the science buildings by comparison.

Anyway, it opened up onto this courtyard with a big green lawn, and this one night in the early spring, I was leaving in the middle of the night, you could see because the moon was out, and as I was walking through the grass, I suddenly noticed around me all these big white rabbits. Hares, I guess. There must have been hundreds of them. All lying on their sides with their feet out, white, and spaced equally apart across the green lawn. It was one of the spookiest things I'd ever seen. They didn't move when I walked through them; I thought about bending down and touching one, but then I thought, what if it didn't move, and I was alone in field full of dead rabbits? Or what if it *did* move? So I just kept moving through them as fast as possible. When I came back in the morning, there was no sign of them. Later, I found out these hares lived all over the university grounds. But nobody I talked to had seen what I had, or anything like this before. I decided it must have been some kind of omen.

So I didn't quite know why I was at school. But it felt good running into one of those campus hares once in a while— against a wall, hunched down and eating its grass. I tried going to mixed parties; by mixed, I mean faculty and graduate students. But these were always boring because nobody could really talk to anybody else, as it would jeopardize his or her *professionalization*. Nobody talked about literature, at least not to me. And if you did, it always felt like you were in a play where, to everyone's embarrassment, you'd shouted out your line at the wrong time across a silent theatre. Mainly the professors complained about their salaries. And anyway, I was wondering what it mattered reading novels about the class struggle in Victorian England. That's when I started getting deeper into the world at the bar, and got more involved with Billy.

I liked to go back into the kitchen of The Rainy Gazebo. It was a funny name because it almost never rained here, and there was nothing pastoral-feeling about the part of town we worked in. But I was happier sitting back there watching Billy make food or clean up than almost anywhere else. Sometimes Jim would swing back with some fancy drinks he'd made up at the bar. It would be silly to compare it to an artist's studio. But it had that private-world feeling to it. Sometimes I felt a kind of satisfied model's boredom, swinging my legs, sketching in Billy's book, and waiting around for him to finish cleaning his cutlery, the cutting surfaces, and the floor.

Mostly, I liked to sit on the steel counter and watch Billy make gourmet pizzas—the way he would pat one down, making its surface really flat. When I ate there, I could always tell if Billy was working, and if he'd made the pizza or shepherd's pie, by how pressed-down and smooth the surface was. I had read an essay about the sculptor Rodin where it said that his clay figures, usually women, always looked messy because Rodin couldn't distinguish between flesh and art. To control one, he had to show his dominance over the other, so he needed to show how his hand had moulded it. Because of this, none of his figures stand out from any of the others, or take the space around them as their own. They look pushed-down, half-finished. Not like they're emerging from the clay, but like they are being forced back into it, like if the hand had continued, they would have disappeared altogether.

I thought of Billy's pizzas this way, but more as the opposite. I always thought of his flat food surfaces as canvas. Billy was a painter, not a sculptor, but he hadn't done a painting in over five years, and it was like he was always trying to find a way back to his art, and away from his life, by working it into his job. Though I'm sure this didn't occur to him. Actually, there was something kind of obscene feeling about a perfectly smooth pizza or shepherd's pie—food that should have some texture to be swallowed.

Sometimes I think Billy fancied he could become a real chef and be artistic that way. But management always rejected his menu ideas. Said they were "country style" and that wasn't what they were going for. They didn't know what they were talking about, Billy said, and once he got furious and took the money for that night's dinner special and went to the mega-supermarket across the street and bought twenty small chickens and made twenty chicken-curry pot pies. When management found out, they made him throw it all out. That was fine with me. I got to eat chicken-curry pot pie at work for a week. It tasted good and that's all that mattered, Billy thought. But as I was chewing, and his eyes gleamed with indignation, I thought of all the nice restaurants I'd eaten at around the world, and about the clever ways people redo simple or rustic dishes by adding a delicate cage of burnt sugar, a long-stemmed berry, or a stick of lemongrass—what's called "vertical interest." I had a friend in culinary school who got a failing grade once because her apple pie didn't have enough "vertical interest," which seems like the wrong thing to ask of an apple pie. But in this case, I thought management was right: Billy's art was not in his cooking.

Still, there was a way in which this routine work made Billy seem more complex. And I came to think of this complexity as existing in the two sides of Billy's hands. In bed, Billy had the particular habit of stroking my face with the back of his hand. Cheeks, forehead, chin, neck. I don't think anyone else had ever done this, except maybe my father when I was a small child. It seemed like an extreme gesture of tenderness to me. But he would also stroke my whole body this way, and it gave me the funny sensation of being touched the way a blind person would touch you to see what you looked like. When it occurred to me, one day, that Billy never actually touched me with the front of his hand, I asked him about it, and he said it was because he couldn't feel anything the normal way anymore. He'd been working in kitchens for so many years, and had burned himself so many times, that his fingertips and palms had lost all their nerve endings.

That sounded kind of romantic to me. Until I realized that he didn't care whether he got burned or not, and for years had been grabbing pans out of the oven with just his bare hands. This was something I couldn't understand, and it made me feel far away from Billy and Jim and the rest of them. So it was right about then that I got the first inkling that the world I'd been playing around in all this time, that I had attached myself to, had its own logic I couldn't follow. And though it was a world that found me as curious as I did it, in the end, it was quite possible that it didn't care about me one bit.

I should have known, then, what it would mean staying

close to that. But it also meant that Billy never judged me, for the scars on my body, or for my toenail that had never grown back properly. He just didn't care, or seem to notice anyway, so I felt pretty comfortable around him, and one time I asked him what he liked, specifically. Billy told me that he liked to spank people. I never had been. Only once, by my dad, when I was about two. My mother said it was one of the funniest things she had ever seen, that you could tell my father didn't want to do it, but that I had to be spanked to learn not to run out in the middle of the road; he put me over his knee very ceremoniously and brought his hand down once, awkwardly, and had a very serious face when he did it. When I asked Billy how he would do it, his eyes lit up with a kind of pleasure and he said hard, with the back of his hand.

"But not too hard," I said.

"No, not too hard," he said.

Part II

So will I turn her virtue into pitch,
And out of her own goodness make the net
That shall enmesh them all.

— **Iago,** *Othello*

You call them sins; I call them decisions.

— **Meryl Streep,** *Ironweed*

It was also around this time that Star-Anise came into the picture. Actually, she had been there all along, but I hadn't known at first. Well, I'd known, but Billy on the couch at 3AM has a way of making you believe only the story at hand, and at hand was me and Billy. So I knew there was a ghost of a girlfriend two provinces over, and I knew better. But I was interested in how a girl, seemingly so important, could disappear in a single moment. Because I had been that girl a number of times, but I hadn't been *this* girl before. The one with the whole story at her fingertips. So, after I let Billy upstairs that first night "to use my washroom," and onto my couch, and after I said, "So I hear you have a girlfriend out there on the Prairies," I let Billy lean in and kiss me.

For a while, all Star-Anise was was her name, and the way Billy said it: serious, but not that often. He just called her "Anise," and said that's what she went by. I didn't like the name; it made me uneasy. Anise's family was straight-up German, and it bothers me when people's names seem pulled from the air or some other place. Like their parents wanted to bless them with something that would take them away from where they'd landed in the world, put them into a fairytale, as if that would help them. Every year, the most common names for babies in America are those of popular soap opera characters. In a Sociology class I took in college, we learned that, statistically, people born into a certain class almost always stay there or move up. But I don't know if that's true, the way things are going. Jim's father was a professor, like mine; Billy's was a shrink of some kind, and here we all were, working in bars. I figured Anise's parents must have been hippies.

At any rate, it was the name of tea and Chinese cooking powders, medicinal oils, and perfume. And, it was nearing Christmas, so the exotic eight-pointed stars were everywhere in the health food stores and the market, which made it hard not to think of her. That, and the fact that pretty soon, Billy felt he could discuss her with me as freely as he did with Jim or any of the regulars at the bar. Sometimes I would tell him not to, because I didn't think it was right; but he'd just start up again anyway, if he was in the mood. It got to be a bother to keep reminding him, so in the end I just let him. And from what Billy told me about the two of them, I got closer than I cared to, to that world I couldn't go down into.

Billy told me about the night he and Anise got together. It was at Blue City, a warehouse-like club downtown. I'd only been to Blue City once or twice. Everything about the place unnerved me. It tried to cover up its general emptiness and hollow feeling with permanent displays of Halloween decorations and other strange things, like fake vines and swaths of felt stapled here and there to the walls and ceiling. I guess it was like a weekend getaway for the kind of people who would never have cottages or money. I'd heard that in the early '80s, it had been the hub of the punk rock scene. DOA had played there a few times. But having a right-wing government in power for nearly forty years must have killed all that anarchism, and now, what seemed like a loop of techno music played most nights, and it was where the

Goths gathered on weekends. Trolling amongst them would be a few army guys, and guys who worked in the oilpatch who were bored and liked to come by to see what the freaks were doing.

The lifers, you could call them, entered in zombie make-up and red-tinted contact lenses, waving glowsticks above their multicoloured hair—cartoon shapes in their tight rubber dresses and platforms, vinyl pants with no ass to them. They carried various instruments of torture around, and it seemed like this was all far more necessary than you'd want it to be, and at the same time very monotonous.

The alternative clubs I'd grown up in, back on the coast, gave you a stylized and evolving sense of everything the big city was about. But Blue City had the on-edge feeling of a small town. Like you arrived there from the Metropolis thinking you knew better, having seen everything, and then everything again in its refined and ironic form... until someone who's grown up there tells you the story about the kid on the high school football team who one day pulled an axe from his duffle bag, ran into the bleachers, and chopped up his parents. That's when you realize you know nothing.

All kinds of stories of passion and betrayal must play themselves out there every weekend in that black hole, but all I could ever make out were bodies in the strobe—frozen and contorted in whiteface around the dancefloor.

Anyway, this was the backdrop to Anise and Billy's love. According to Billy, he'd been pursuing Anise around Blue City for nine years, with no luck. Then, one night, Anise got drunk and fell down the back stairs. She broke her leg, the bone right through. Billy was the first person she called, from the bottom of the stairs. Maybe she was thinking of his mother. Since then, Anise and Billy had been together.

In my arms, Billy would recall that early time with Anise with joy: how, back home after a night at the club, she would appear from behind the room divider—coming at him with her smiling, open self and four or five bottles between her fingers, that they'd drink the bottom out of 'til daylight.

Well, as it turned out, that fall wasn't fate. From then on, and maybe even before, Anise was always falling down. You could explain that this had to do with her height. She was even taller than Billy. He liked women being taller than him. She must have been over six feet tall, taller in her platform boots, and she seemed even thinner than Billy, too. She had narrow hips and broad, bony shoulders—something Billy once said he admired in me—and thin arms that fell from them, or would stretch out, animated, all around her. And she had a million costumes, he said. At the club, sometimes she would appear as a geisha in a tight silken dress, black eyelids, and a long black wig with a red flower in it, fingernails to match, and a little paper umbrella. For Valentine's Day, she'd strapped on a set of towering angel wings made of raven-like feathers, which she wore with a velvet corset, ripped black fishnets and elbow-length gloves. Billy himself did not bother with costumes, though he was mesmerized by and admired Anise's theatre; Billy only cut his hair or bought a new shirt from Army & Navy when absolutely necessary.

There were these few things, but for the most part, long stretches would go by and I wouldn't hear a thing about Anise. Then, some morning over breakfast, Billy would tell me that Anise had fallen down and fractured her hip. She'd been on vacation, running with a dog along the beach, and now was in traction in a hospital in Ontario. Back then, these breaks were the only times I really considered Anise. Billy's interest seemed honed then. I wasn't jealous, but I'd been trying to help Billy better himself, and these small, repeated crises seemed to hold them to each other in some way that was distracting.

The only other way Anise was present had to do with Billy's bed. It was the one place I wasn't allowed, and the door to his room was usually closed. It seemed funny to me, this rule; it was an ugly little mattress and the only piece of furniture in his room. Besides, we went at it everywhere else, more than once on the filthy floor of the kitchen at The Gazebo.

Billy didn't know it, but one night, when I was still too drunk to go home, I woke up on his sofa wrapped in a dirty-white knitted blanket made by somebody's grandmother long ago, and I went in and lay down next to him. There, all around the bed, low down on the walls and crammed next to each other, were dozens of pictures of Anise. Every direction you looked: right behind your head, your foot, and if you turned on either of your sides. It was like Bluebeard's closet, or like one of those cop shows where the killer collects pictures of his victim. But at the time, I almost felt pity for Billy; there was a desperation to it, like he had no memory, so he had to keep it all on the wall.

I haven't mentioned yet that Anise has some kind of disease of the blood that may or may not be killing her. Maybe that's why she could vanish from Billy's mind like magic when he needed her to. Though... it was probably also what drew him. I would forget too, until Billy would casually mention over dinner that Anise had been tearing her hair out that day, and I would have to put down my fork. It wasn't humiliating or anything; Anise was the dark-eyed girl in the photographs. That was fine with me. I was happy with everything staying as it was. When Billy went to visit her, he disappeared. When he got back, we were together.

But I was interested in these pictures. There was one of Anise and Billy smooshed together cheek to cheek with a country road and some old stone building behind them. Like they wanted it to be some place far away and mystical, though it was probably just some suburb of Winnipeg. Anise turned into this mysticism herself, when she wasn't at the club deliberately dressed as a crack whore. On hikes through the mountains, she wore elaborate earrings and wide-armed, flowing, Eastern-y clothing. In one photo, she's on her knees on a mountain peak, bending back in a way that means she does yoga: holding onto her heels, her upturned flat stomach filling with God, sunshine, chakras, whatever. I guess that helped with her sickness. On her long, strong-looking hand she has pressed across Billy's chest, there are a number of thick and bejeweled silver rings, including one on her thumb.

The thing you noticed most about her, though, was her hair, which she kept in a high, impressive ponytail above those broad, straight shoulders. By the way it blew across her body, all tendrilly, you could tell it fell all the way down her back. Her short, killer bangs made it look even longer. She was like a princess and a horse at once. All that positive flow seemed to enter Billy; in the pictures, it was on his face, like a borrowed happiness. But I could ignore that. I lay there a while longer and studied the face of the girl.

Before Billy, I'd never been with a man who had a girlfriend already, even though men have, more than once, confided in me that they've woken to see my face superimposed over the one sleeping next to them. I know that sometimes a man will buy the same perfume for his girlfriend and his lover, to avoid confusion. And these are the kind of things that make a woman study another woman's face and clothes and movements, looking for the thing he's seen in both that they don't see themselves. It can make a woman feel like a stranger to herself.

But I wasn't worried about this. I knew what it was that Billy thought he saw, but I also knew I was different from Anise. Like I said, it wasn't that I was jealous. There was something to her, though, something big, even regal-like, that made you want to get ahold of it. And since I don't paint, it's more I was interested in describing Anise the way Billy would, if he could.

He always said I was better with words than him. And even though you couldn't say Billy was a great painter, he had a talent for arrangement and peculiar details. And I admired that.

It must have been why he liked Anise so much. She was like a creature that has a bit of every other creature in her, too. The princess-horse face: squarish, fine and long. But unusual eyes also. Like a bird of prey's: flat on the top and a solid brown, that sometimes went black and serious, blind-looking and sunk with everything at once. Her nose was also interesting: curved falcon-like, with a small diamond stud in it that you could see when she tipped her head into the bar light, one knuckle under her chin, her overbite pulled down in thought. A lot of times Anise posed for the camera, looking happy and strong; but in these candid Blackhoof photos, her expression was fierce and frightened at once. It gave her, even more so, the look of a bird of prey in a dwindling environment.

All of this I gathered while Billy slept beside me. Later, I found out the seedy little mattress belonged to Anise. Something she had left behind for Billy when she moved away, which was why I wasn't allowed on it. It was as though Anise had drawn some kind of line. That Billy went along with it was part of the logic I didn't understand. It seemed like the kind of crumb you looked for in wartime or something. A contract two people agree upon, but that only makes sense in the middle of insanity. But maybe it was also the kind of crumb that can sustain people for a long time. Amongst all the photos of Anise there had been one of her and Billy's two clenched fists, knuckles fitted tightly together like a joint.

The months away from everything to do with my future went by like this: in the kitchen with Billy, and drinking after hours at the bar. I'd pour him beers in the afternoon, after he'd brought me a breakfast burrito for my Saturday afternoon shift. We'd talk a bit about art or the politics of the industry. If something had happened on the Avenue, or in the local news, we'd talk about that. How there was a serial cat killer on the loose. Or how some minister had slipped up, saying that all the foreigners coming in had better vote the way Albertans always had if they knew what was good for them. Most of our foreigners, though, were what the government called "temporary workers." Billy had a guy named Nadif, from Somalia, working with him in the kitchen. And even though he was probably a doctor in his country, Billy thought he was doing him a big favour by training him how to cook a pizza, throwing him a few extra shifts or an extra five in tips. I used to watch Nadif just stare at the dough. He quit before too long, and I think he went back home.

Often, it was the cops we talked about. Like when the playoffs were on and they were locking up teenagers just for jaywalking and pushing over garbage cans. And then there was that famous incident of the woman who'd sworn at a cop. She'd been handcuffed and thrown facedown on sidewalk in what the officer called self-defence. A journalist had photographed the whole thing, but the cop got away with it. It was pretty common, too, for young girls in bars on the Ave to get drugs in their drinks and then get charged for things they didn't remember. Last month, on his way home from the bar, Boris found a girl in the bushes just off the Ave, naked and unable to stand up. She didn't know her name or where she was. She just kept saying, "Don't touch me." The cops were never around for stuff like that. Boris waited an hour with her before they showed.

But it's not like there's any protest to people in this town. When a recently retired MP was caught drunk-driving with a glove compartment full of blow, the local news showed clips of people on the street saying how he was just human, and how hard it must be to join the rest of us again. He ended up with a five-hundred-dollar fine. But most people on the Ave knew what it was like with the cops here, and the news, and the politicians. Ever since the mayor had come up with the term "aggressive panhandler," and the media had run with it, you saw the backwards-baseball-hatted suburbanites and their girlfriends going after The Poor, screaming at them and turning over their bikes and smashing their carts. Stuff like that.

When Billy and I weren't on about the Ave, we'd go to the library or see a movie. Usually after work, Billy would come over to my place. He'd lie down on my floor and say he could finally feel his mind calm down. I'd lie on the carpet in the TV light, up against Billy's bony spine, stoned and gesturing at some infomercial drama that I was analyzing for him. "You're so smart," he'd say, and roll over, his mouth on my mouth, and

I'd run my hand along his thin, tattooed arm and hold onto the sharp bone of his shoulder. We could stay like that for quite a while. That was always enough with Billy. It was all I'd been looking for, I think. I could wait long stretches, months, or years for moments like this.

"But why me?" he finally asked one day, the beer taps between our faces. I could see what he meant. But I'd also seen how a woman lays claim to a man, the one she can make babies with. Getting jobs that afford them trips to Europe, then houses: the kind with *two* sinks in the bathroom, stainless steel appliances and granite counters in the kitchen, 'cause you're supposed to want that. Their life stories were over in one fell swoop. It was such a relief for them to be done with it.

But I'd always stayed away from anything that looked like it would unfold this way. Still, how could I tell Billy? That I loved him the way a painter loves a fine line that replaces a weak and delicate backbone; for the imprint he makes in a room—a stark figure before you, angrily tapping away at something. It was the same with everything: art, writing, men. My preference was for bone over meat. I like things pared down. Irreducible.

But things didn't stay like that.

One Saturday afternoon, I looked up from a pour and the girl in the photographs was sitting behind the taps. Billy hadn't mentioned that Anise was in town. There was the long face, and the large bony thumb with the thick silver ring on it, tilting a Guinness. I recall the pint looking like black water beneath

Anise's eyes, that were like seaman's eyes: watching but not seeing what was right before them in the dark. I was the thing in the water she couldn't see. The anonymous waitress... just to the left. Below the bar, I wiped the white ooze of head from the side of her glass.

I suppose a certain kind of person would get a thrill from this, the two of us brought together this way. Something was bound to happen, finally. Some rising action, some kind of scene. But it wasn't how I'd imagined things—a study of mine coming to life like this: undoing its coat, taking off its snowy hat and whacking it on the bar while asking me for a beer. I'd gotten used to the fixed images. She was with Dara, one of Billy's homely female friends who was half in love with him, and would buy his beers when I wouldn't, or when Anise was out of town. Billy was a classic mooch. I figured Dara pretty much knew what was going on, but like most of Billy's friends, she had made the calculation and chosen to ignore it. It was funny that Anise thought she was her friend.

I started to wonder how long they were going to sit there when all of a sudden, Billy walked in, fast as usual, with his hands in his pockets. Instead of stopping when he reached us, like a director, he whispered a few words into Anise's ear. "OK," her voice trailed off, and we all stared at Billy's back as he crashed out the back door into the deep snow.

A week or so went by and Billy didn't come in, and seemed to have sort of disappeared. But Anise started showing up every second day or so. Like she'd taken over the job. She knew how to use her height, her limbs, and her impressive fall of ponytail when she entered a room. You never got tired of it. It reminded me of an interview I'd seen with a model who said the best advice he ever got was: wherever you are, look like you don't want to be there. That's how Anise looked a lot of the time. Even after she knew everything, she kept coming into The Blackhoof, acting like it was a big faux pas that I'd chosen to have my shift that night. She'd roll in on her long, straight up-and-down legs, spread 'em at the bar, her hands half in her pockets like maybe she was going to shoot somebody and maybe she wasn't.

Day after day, I kept waiting for it all to blow up, for something to happen. But it didn't. Instead came the period I began to see Billy and Anise really together. One afternoon, me and Jim were smoking out front of The Gazebo and they strode right on by, in unison, like two Giacometti figures. Billy waved at us as casual as a brush pass over a chalkboard.... A few days later, I saw Anise by herself. She passed me in broad daylight on the busy Ave, all her hair pulled back from her face that was passionate and bright with tears. A few weeks later, I went for my morning coffee at The Ordinary and there they were, gazing at each other over a table like they were in France or something. Billy drawing Anise's long, pale portrait over and over again in his beat-up sketchbook.

I'd never been a sitter for Billy. He never asked, but also it hadn't occurred to me. When I meet a man, he usually drops whatever meager artistic efforts he occasionally pursues. But ever since Anise was back, Billy was sketching again. He had quit, or been fired from, The Gazebo, and was working at another kitchen downtown. One of those new places that have a wine bar attached. But based on its name, I doubt anyone ever went in. Some genius who'd made it big in the oilpatch had decided to open a chi-chi place to bring all his douchebag oil money friends to, and had called it Wine'd Up. That's really what it was called; his oversight being anyone who knows anything about wine also knows how to use an apostrophe in a non-douchebag way.

Anyway, somehow Billy had convinced the owner to hang a show of his paintings. A flyer had been casually left on the bar of The Hoof. One night only. Judging from the flyer, it was the night before the official opening. I guess, like everyone else, the owner had taken pity on Billy. I could just imagine all of his friends there, looking at the half-dozen unframed canvases they'd already seen about a million times, their edges frayed and grubby from being hauled across the country, apartment to apartment, for the last five years.

To be fair, it sounded like he was trying to crank out some new ones. Jim said Billy'd come home from work one night and tried to finish a canvas, but fell pissing drunk on it instead; when he woke up and realized he'd ruined it, he smashed it into pieces. The next night, when he got home from the kitchen, he found Anise had taken the broken pieces and made a shelf out of them, and put it up on the empty wall of his bedroom. Which was, at least, useful. That's a thing I would never do, as interesting a gesture as it was. Like I said, Anise was committed to this world, wanted to make a home in it. To me it was like she'd decided to build a nest on the dull end of a lightning bolt.

All this to say, I was beginning to realize I was in a funny position: neither quite inside nor quite outside the story. If I were a con man, somehow my mark had gotten away on me, was working the neighbourhood with his own schemes. Billy thought he was running the show; and there I stood, at the side of the stage, like an understudy catching glimpses of the star-crossed lovers, the new true talent blooming beneath the bright lights of the Ave. It was beginning to dawn on me that Billy had made me part of his theatre, a minor character you throw in for a while to accomplish some effect, like a card you pick up and throw away as your hand requires.

Still, I couldn't exactly walk away, leave it alone, and Billy knew this. His schemes depended on the other person's sense of justice. So, despite my raised eyebrow, my stepping back, I was held to his stage: I alone could reveal what Billy was capable of—his duplicity. And yet, if I did—despite the fact I was, as Billy always said, "better than him with words"—I knew it would somehow work against me. Billy would simply roll his baleful eyes and repeat, to whomever it was, the story of his father and his tragic childhood. Billy surrounded himself with the weak and the too-good-of-heart, the easily duped. "You never gave him a chance," Anise later said to me. "You turned them all against him." The truth was, I hadn't said a word around the bar about Billy; and Anise always seemed to be looking the other way whenever Billy pushed to the front of the line to narrow his eyes at me in a filthy look of, what? Triumphant scorn, or the kind one con man might give another—a call to play.

If Billy and I were in battle, Anise, or whatever it was she stood in for, was our ground. I should have seen from the start what a shallow ground it was. The way Billy played her, she was the girl spinning in her costumes and photographing herself, making a record, and thinking of herself as a nineteenth-century tragic heroine. I'd seen her on a stool at The Hoof, her back to me, checking her watch and then taking down her long hair and spreading it about her bare shoulders, just before Billy was done his shift and due to come in. With Billy, Anise was the kind of girl who said things like "But when is love ever easy?" and left it at that.

You see, even though Anise played the part, it was me to whom Billy confessed his dark soul. "I enjoy creating drama," Billy once told me, as we sat cross-legged at the bar, enjoying a pint, while Anise was at work.

"Why?" I asked.

"Just for the sake of it," he said.

I knew he trusted me alone with this; Billy saw me as a kind of partner. I also knew if I betrayed this, if I tried to expose Billy, he would play on my female pain. I would become part of his lie-filled theatre where there was no exit: it would wrap itself around me like it does a starlet, until I no longer knew the difference between the role and myself—just like what happened to Anise. No, I knew what I had to do. To stay on the outside, I had to become the moral person. This meant doing nothing. I had to keep the special knowledge of Billy's deceit to myself. "Thank god that's not me," I had to keep in mind. I think I learned all this from Shakespeare.

At my university, to fill a certain English requirement, you took either Shakespeare or Milton. You needed only one of them to graduate. If you weren't on the ball you'd end up with a year of Paradise. Every term, I'd sort of forgot I was going back, so I only ever got the first week of Shakespeare, hoping the undecided, or maybe just the skeptical, ahead on the waiting list would give up.

Despite twelve long books and months of Milton, the only things I can recall about Paradise are the Devil's sparkling eyes, the "darkness visible," and the thing about how the mind is its own place that can make a hell out of heaven, or vice versa. Which I think I bought back then, but wasn't too sure about anymore. I'd been living in Alberta for seven years, so I was pretty sure it was the place that made a hell of the mind.

But I'd read *Othello,* and the return of Shakespeare each term was what taught me this useful thing: that in tragedy, the one who is outside the action, the one who's in the audience, is the one who gets to take the moral position. And so I decided the reverse must be true, too: by being the moral person, I could get outside of the drama, go back to observation and doing my job. And so, after several weeks of being nowhere, I tracked Billy down and broke it off. I was discreet about it—I thought of it as a last gesture of love. And as the moral one, I had no interest in ruining anyone's life.

Besides, I'd finished my writing and had defended it, and would be convocating in a few months. It had taken me long enough; unfortunately, I'd been under the impression that a master's degree meant something, so I'd spent six years on it. Everyone said it was too bad I hadn't turned it into a PhD.

I could even think to myself that Billy and his life had helped me finish my final chapter. Sometimes I even thought this was why I'd stayed with Billy. In it, I analyzed a novel about a group of destitute inner-city people. My argument was: even though these characters never escape their wretched lives, there's real hope and power in the book's rebellious grammar and structure. I explained all this to Billy, and suggested that maybe he could stay away from The Blackhoof for a while, just a few weeks, while I was on shift, and that eventually everything would even out. Billy nodded in agreement. After all, I was more than fair: letting him off the hook and keeping quiet. And I was sure that in a few months, everything would be back to normal.

The next night, when I looked up, Billy was in front of my station, unwrapping his long scarf from around his neck and not acknowledging me as he settled himself down at the bar in the manner he always did. He was with Suzette, whom I'd talked to only a couple times as a regular. Pretty soon they were all comfy at the wood, drinking their nice-looking pints, in close conversation, Suzette's fingers in her long, shiny black hair.

When I bother looking up at the regulars during a shift, there are moments I wonder what stories they're telling each other, night after night—each one with his or her own particular tragedy. I wondered now, while lifting the beer glasses from the revolving dishwasher steam and placing them on the mat in front of Billy as he humiliated me. I'd misjudged him, how far he would go. Billy was, I realized, willing to risk love, reputation, everything, for the drama he was putting on—for no other reason than to see how it would unfold.

From then on, when I didn't see Billy for a while, I knew Anise was in town; and when Anise left again, Billy and I would be back together. He had replaced all other men for me, all other kinds of beauty. He was unkempt. Dirty, even. His hair. His feet and lower legs had a rash, perhaps from standing in the heat and humidity of the kitchen in the same shoes every day. And he was constantly rubbing his hands and ankles together like a cricket. I suppose, also, his liver wasn't doing too well. With some, you can smell the poison fighting with the flesh. Those ones can fill up an entire filthy city bus with the smell of failure; you think of their humanity as their inside organs. You can almost taste, in the close, foul air, how long they have left.

But Billy's humanity didn't smell of anything, and he had a skin that was unreal. In the smooth, narrow valley of his stomach, there was a small, perfect belly button, as though it had been scooped out in a flourish by a slim blade. Altogether a transparency that wasn't sickness, like some people said of him, but like the ricepaper around a salad roll. There was an art to it. You could glimpse the blue, otherworldly rivers running beneath in many places. After ten pints of ale, Billy would lie there, patient like that other world, with his eyes closed and fingers folded across his chest as I moved my pathetic, correct mouth over him.

I broke up with Billy twice more. Each time, he had something new to say, to keep me. It was never convincing—Billy was a hack when it came to storytelling; and like he always said, I was better with words than him. But his persistence reminded me of something I'd been fighting since I was a little girl.

My parents had done all the right things. Gymnastics, horseback riding, then ice-skating at the rink on Saturday mornings, the same Carpenters song playing year after year: "Why do birds suddenly appear..." I hated skating, the synthetic skirts, the combined smells of stale ice and boys' sweat in the rough cement; the garish, bashed-up boards of hockey. But I kept going, got better at it, as expected.

Later, in Europe, I'd see some things other little girls would never see. A young Berlin soldier held out his hand to help me up the black, wrought iron steps of a train. I learned how to order ice cream in Italian, eat it from chilled metal cups. It was delicious, then gone. Then it was on to another beautiful thing.

I learned to take the mundane with the exceptional, the ugly with the beautiful—none of it belonged to me. I had discovered nothing on my own. I couldn't remember the names of places we travelled to, or how we got there, only the images. As I got older, I watched other people find their passions, or at least settle on the things that made sense to them. I, however, went on to whatever thing was next—for a while thinking it would bring me, finally, to some place.

At times, I imagined a canary-yellow kitchen with a butcher's block, lush hanging plants, and a black-and-white tile floor. I must have been in a kitchen like this once. But this is all I ever thought of the future, this room; and always, whatever path I chose next would eventually end.

Now, as happened every few years—with this or that person, a cause, a vocation—here was something demanding I take it as my own chosen thing. I'd seen it fail with all the others before. I watched the strength of hope and excitement die in their eyes as they discovered what I had known from the start. After they left, their love thinned out in my mind and was forgotten. I got used to being the answer so often, for so many.

The unlikelihood, the grotesqueness, that it was Billy was what drove me. And one afternoon, at a table in The Rainy Gazebo, about an hour before Anise was due to show up, I heard myself telling Billy that I loved him. As soon as I said it, it felt true. Perfectly true and deceptive at once.

Part III

My, but you slay me
In my rainy gazebo tree.

— **Kristin Hersh**, *"Gazebo Tree"*

Something was sure to happen now. It must. Christmas was approaching, again, and Anise had been in town for nearly three months this time. Billy told me that they had made plans to fly to Anise's parents for the holidays. Three days later, after I'd told Billy I loved him, it was the Blackhoof's fifteenth anniversary party. In the middle of the festivities, as my eyes adjusted to the darkness and silver paper, Billy appeared, sitting drunk as a lord at a corner table. He pulled me in and his mouth found my mouth and there was the sweetness in the shiny darkness and that was all. He wasn't going, would never leave me again. He whispered to me: "Wait until she's gone." When I turned around, the room was full of his cohorts talking and laughing and seeing nothing.

A couple of days later, just before Billy was supposed to leave, he came into the bar with Mike, one of the brothers from his father's other family. Mike, like his sister, was pretty religious, and they were hell-bent on unifying the family. The day after the party, I had wandered into an antiquarian bookstore on the Avenue and found a signed hardcover copy of a book Billy had taken out of the library about a million times. It was of art done during the First World War. Billy liked it because all the paintings were of the battlefield, done by young Canadian soldiers who weren't trained to paint or draw, who didn't know if they were going to see anything beyond that particular hill or muddy hole again, but had to put on paper what they were seeing. Billy's father had done some such sketches in Vietnam.

After I'd bought it, I was walking along the Ave towards The Blackhoof when suddenly I thought of my mother and how she would always spoil my father and me at Christmastime with a rare edition of a book or photograph, a luxurious pair of pajamas. My mother had been what she called "dirt poor" growing up, and whatever crisis or betrayal had happened during the year would be forgiven in that moment with her exuberant and expensive gesture of love coming out of the paper.

The bar was pretty quiet and I could hear the wrapping rustle as I held the present over the wood to Billy. He opened it and, with a measured gesture of enthusiasm, thanked me, bobbing his head in a sort of formal way. "That's quite a lovely gift," Mike added. As Billy folded the paper, he told me that he couldn't see me that night, as planned, as Anise had a staff Christmas party he had to go to.

The next day, I left my apartment early and began walking the Avenue. I knew if I looked in enough places, I would find one of them. At such times, I get a feeling of certainty. Besides, there was a limited number of places Billy could be. A little farther east of The Blackhoof was a bar called The Emperor. The Avenue had gotten pretty rough over the last few years: the city wouldn't put a limit on the number of bars in the area, despite public concern. So the well-heeled hipsters and semi-professionals who were once Blackhoof regulars had moved up to the quieter end of the Ave, and to The Emperor.

Skulls of horses and wild animals hung on the red walls, faux crystal chandeliers ran down the centre of the barroom; all the tables were made of rough wood, but were also stylish. It was an ironic variation of what you might call "Prairie Riche." Like when you went to the symphony to hear Rachmaninoff and you had to walk around a red sports car being raffled off in the foyer. Or you go to an expensive restaurant in the mall and women in thousand-dollar suits are drinking red and blue martinis. That's "Prairie Riche."

Billy saw me come in, but kept talking to the random suit standing next to him, the only other person in the place at 2:30 in the afternoon. He looked like he was trying to strike a deal of some kind. I ordered a Negra Modelo and sat at the other end of the bar. I like Modelo, the unusual shape of the brown bottle and the gold-and-black foil label. Billy was taking his time getting around to me, so after I'd killed half my beer, I left. I was most of the way back to The Blackhoof before he was beside me, his hands in his pockets, walking with his fast, jerky steps.

"So that it? You've quit talking?" Billy had a funny way of enunciating every syllable very correctly and sonorously, while also slurring all his words. When I didn't answer, he started talking fast, for Billy. I didn't hear a lot of it. We'd stopped outside the 7-Eleven. Billy was pleading with me, trying out different versions of how things had gone, putting forth resolutions, promises of a future: to wait until after Christmas. "I'll be with you 100%," he said. In the greyish day, his face looked afflicted—screwed up in the lie, maybe some truth of it. The thing was, I didn't know what Billy wanted. It was like there was an insistence in him, but no goal. But I was pretty sure he was still flying east. So why was he in front of me, rubbing his legs together with exceptional vigour and talking fast? After all, there was always going to be someone else for Billy, someone to believe his stories and try to make a happy ending out of them.

As I stood there, watching him in some sort of pain, the two sides of Billy's hands began turning in my head, and I became very aware of some electrical activity in my brain— like something from one side trying to zap its way over to the other. There haven't been many times in my life when I've felt I had to do something in a moment in order to survive. I mean, I hadn't spent a lot of time in the woods; I'd never been up north or anything. Even on a daily basis, I take way fewer risks than most people: I look in every direction before changing a lane or crossing a street. I never eat things more than a day past their expiration date. But I figured that's how I'd lasted this long. So it was a new feeling suddenly upon me: the moment you decide whether you're going to go further, accept love like the back of a hand.

In that moment, I found myself choosing what one might call the moral universe; I guess I'd reached the border to that other world and decided I wasn't crossing. I was finally really leaving Billy. "It's over," I said. The common line came out of me and was immediately whipped away by a speeding monster truck with a backwards-baseball-hatted boy hanging out of it. In its wake, the moral universe appeared to be a crappy little intersection of sagging storefronts buttressed by plots of grey snow.

I turned from Billy's tense, anticipating body and continued on down the Ave. It was midday and I thought about how my face must look. A lot of families were out doing their weekend wandering, so I decided on the first side street. There was nothing you could buy on the Avenue that you could actually use: you had to drive to the mall for a decent spatula. Later that night, the same few blocks would be threaded with the grandsons of farmers, drunk and wrecking stuff, maybe hitting someone's skull from behind with a beer bottle before racing their trucks back to the suburbs. In the morning, you'd have to make your way around the patches of frozen vomit.

Now, if there needs to be a climax to all this, you could say what happened next was the lead-up to it. The street I'd just turned down, just on the other side of the tracks from the 7-Eleven, was one I normally didn't walk down, and I passed a store I'd never really paid attention to before. For no reason, I looked up at the sign swinging from two chains. It said Artifactual. The word played in my head and I remembered Billy saying Anise worked at a place with a similar sounding name: a chic-er place, downtown. But in the same second, I knew, as I turned my head, that this was the place, and sure enough, there was Anise, bowing to straighten something behind the dark storefront glass. Now, why did I turn down that street just then, and what were the chances of Anise being in the window? If you happened to be looking out of it, you could catch everything happening outside the 7-Eleven. We'd been working a block away from each other for months. When I tell people that part, they say it sounds like something from a movie. Naturally, I opened the door and went in.

The place was narrow but went deep into the building. The sides were lined with meager offerings: dusty woven things were nailed to the wall, a dumb-looking human sculpture squatted in the entrance. Shiny scarves and pillows were strewn about in someone's notion of a marketplace in India or Africa. But it was the import boutique you see in every city, in the mall, on the side streets of small towns, giving the lower middle-class a taste of the Exotic, the dribble-down of an outdated colonialism.

Anise stood there in the midst of it, her face bored, fixed like a guard's. She was tall as an Egyptian goddess in black knee-high goth boots, accented in African wood jewelry, and she wore a dark one-piece Japanese outfit, admittedly elegant; it was something I would wear. Behind her there was a second room; you could see it through a gaping curtain with tiny gold elephants on it. I glimpsed a maze of wood display cabinets pushed together— overstock, presumably: the same unremarkable jewelry as up front, small carvings of giraffes, Buddhas, and the like. Nevertheless, I needed to get behind that elephant curtain like it was the sesame door to 1,001 nights. With what I hoped was the air of a blasé shopper I slowly edged my way past Anise, like you would a sleeping dragon, or a griffin. Along a mile of cabinet, I kept my head down, moved carefully, all the while trying to look interested in the cliché crap on display.

Just when I'd made it to the back room, the bells over the door jingled. Anise welcomed someone with a grand "Hi!" but not like you would a customer, and Billy's downer voice said something back. Right away, things began moving in my head. Should I stay there? I wandered about the maze of trinkets for a minute or two. No, instead... instead, I decided it was time for the stage. I took a breath and came out from behind the curtain.

Anise, I could tell, was facing me. Billy, I could see from the corner of my eye, had his back to me still. I was a stone's throw from him, whatever that is; I could throw something and it would hit him, at any rate. I stood by a display and waited. I peered at a little carved Buddha. Nothing happened. I bent inquisitively towards the crude little thing like it was a marvelous treasure. *Not a thing was happening.* Finally, I had to look up.

With that, everything was set into motion, came together like it had been written that way. Anise moved towards Billy, draping her long arm over his shoulders with the easy fanfare of an actress greeting an admirer she thinks is beneath her. She said: "I've been online. I've found you a flight for a hundred dollars less"—unaware, apparently, that Billy had left her, and would not be meeting the folks this Christmas. There might have been, it's possible, a slight fall in Billy's shoulders, but he recovered quickly enough. In each of his hands was a coffee from the 7-Eleven. Billy and I had, it appeared, been acting out different scenes. My freshly executed swan song was, for Billy, only an inconvenient interlude: an irritating delay in the purchasing of Anise's afternoon coffee... something he probably did every day around 3 o'clock before turning the corner to see me at 3:30. Billy handed one of the still-steaming coffees to Anise and gave her skinny ass a squeeze, quick and jaunty, so the other saleswoman wouldn't see. But I saw. From behind "the fourth wall," I, the unacknowledged customer, saw everything in those few moments. Anise responded by swaying into him. It reminded me of the photo of Anise and Billy's pressed-together knuckles; the world was meant to see their two bony bodies as one. But Anise was turned the wrong way. The other saleswoman wasn't her true audience, I was... because I knew something was, in fact, between them. Not Billy, nor Anise, nor The Other Saleswoman had all the pieces. Only I had—it was just as I'd said I'd wanted.

In a play, this is how the truth is revealed—a technique that might make the modern reader say, "Oh, come on!" But in life, the chance of time and place and action converging so tidily is a gift from the Fates, a serious call to action. So I didn't take my exit then. Instead, I continued to hover there, my head in the cabinet. "May I help you?" Anise said over Billy's shoulder, finally acknowledging me, her customer. "Just looking," I heard myself say; it rang out like my only line. I didn't look up to see how Billy reacted when he heard my voice and realized I was there with them. But I could feel the stage beneath them widen to reach me. And I heard Anise whisper "Okay" to him in that permissive way from before, and Billy disappeared like some old-time villain out the jingling door.

Anise went back to chatting with the other saleswoman. I wandered about the store awhile more—awash, you might say, with tragic revelation. I knew I couldn't keep it up for long, though, without looking like a crazy woman plotting to run off with a sackload of small wood giraffes. Also, I was shaking a bit. I didn't feel the raised eyebrow, then, or the stepping back; I was right up cold against the thing I knew I should do.

Still, when do you ever really know if that moment of decision has arrived? Can't it always be postponed—the moment you change the course of everything with a few unremarkable words? I had no rehearsed soliloquy. Eventually I left Artifactual, like I was closing a book on it all, and I began walking the direction I'd been heading in before. At the corner, there was a nice-looking bench outside a small community theatre. I sat on it and looked at the clumps of grey snow for a while. "If I were Anise, I would want to know" was the line that finally came to me, in what sounded like my dead mother's voice, and it made me get up and go back to the store.

Anise was in the spot I'd left her, still talking to the other saleswoman. I said her name: "Anise." She turned and looked like she was trying to figure out how she knew this girl.

"I need to talk to you about Billy," I said.

"Okay," she said.

I looked for a ripple of suspicion, of anything, crossing her face. Nothing. You could see how Billy did it. I took her behind the elephant curtain, and in the dusty maze of crap made in China, I stood under the towering Anise and I told her.

She was calm. She was gracious. She thanked me. Like a slow detective, she asked a few questions. About the mattress. We had both been with men like Billy before, we laughed wryly about that. And that was it. She thanked me again and I left. "If there's anything else you need to know, you know where to find me," I said. If I'd had a business card, I probably would have given it to her. When I got home, the phone was ringing, but I didn't answer it. I knew it was Billy.

Part IV

Tragedy, to be felt as such, requires a temporary exemption from daily life—a compassionate leave—which the modern city does not grant.

— **John Berger**, *"Ralph Fasanella and the Experience of the City"*

About a month passed, easily, after that day at the 7-Eleven. I hadn't seen or heard a thing from Billy and Anise. It was like they had disappeared. I felt a great relief about the whole thing. You could even say a feeling of contentment had come over me. Then, one Saturday afternoon, Anise came into the bar. She ordered a Guinness from me. I asked her if she was all right and took her money and put her pint down in front of her. Her eyes were fierce and dark as usual, but focused this time, on me. Her lips were pierced and lined in pencil in a way that made her mouth look small and aged her. We were both approaching our mid-thirties; you could begin to see what we'd look like as

older women.

She took her pint and sat way down at the end of the bar. I came by after a bit and asked her if she wanted another. "Don't you feel any remorse?" she said with a passion that startled me. It struck me as a grand word to use. Very particular. I told her of course I did. That's why I'd come to see her. What more could I do for her? Besides, you could tell it was a question she'd saved for Billy, and maybe it hadn't been answered right. I knew by now that Billy was a man who had said "I'm sorry" a million times over in his life.

But that word she used got me thinking. In a tragedy, remorse means there's some final reckoning, some sort of self-recognition—an end that promises a new beginning, at least for the person watching. And there's a certain satisfaction in that. But how often does that happen in life?

A few weeks earlier, the great playwright Harold Pinter had died, and so they replayed an old interview with him on TV. In it, he says that truth and lies can never be separated in fiction, but always should be in life. This seemed to say something about how a person should act in life, but also how morality shouldn't be put on art.

Shakespeare seemed to suggest something similar about life—but he did it in his plays. His evil characters are the ones who can't tell the difference between life and a play, truth and illusion. At best, they're pretty much doomed. Iago makes a foolish spectacle of everyone who's trusted him in the "play" he tricks them into. And that's what he thinks of life, that people can be fooled into any story. Othello brings about a tragedy based on these far-fetched stories. Macbeth, in his hour of dark revelation, claims that the world's a stage you walk about alone, until phzzt, you're rubbed out like a tealight.

"I need proof," Anise said, leaning over the bar. "Billy's all I have, and he's saying things different from what you told me." I had the proof. Not that I expected Anise and I would collapse in death throes together, vindicated in the exposure of Billy's lies. But I had the kind that would make the pieces fall into place. In life, usually you don't have the courage, and the time for proof passes; or, you can't be bothered. Most of the time, everyone just keeps going and nobody can really tell when they've learned a lesson, when something's over, what's real, or when the truth is revealed.

But I was an English major and knew that the immutable law of a great tragedy was this recognition or discovery. It's in the old tragedies that things come to light; and like I said, even if everyone's lying around dead on the floor, there's some kind of hope in that. Proof is the only thing that can lead to the purity of remorse, and remorse undoubtedly leads to some change for the better. Lady Macbeth can't wash the blood from her hands, but she gives it a try; she knows the consequences. In a bar, a person washes her hands a hundred times a night, and every surface over and over. But she never manages to get past the top layer of filth, which is always back the next day anyway, and it doesn't matter. So maybe in the end, Harold Pinter was wrong, and it's better to model your life after a fiction, a work of literature; that's the only place people know the difference between truths and lies.

Everything I'd learned from my English classes was in the back of my mind, I guess, and so I thought I was doing the best thing when I told Anise I'd meet her the next day at The Ordinary and give her a letter Billy had written me. For now, I gave her what I had; from my keychain, I unclipped the small clock Billy had given to me as a graduation present, and tossed it down the bar to her. She fingered it for a moment. I didn't see what she did with it.

The next day at The Ordinary, Anise showed up twenty minutes late. I handed her the letter:

Hey Riel,

I went to the clinic and it turns out that it's just axema. So I got some cream for it. Anise visited my work last night. I explained that I have been dealing with a greater sense of depression, and she understands. After christmas we will try to relax and not put our expectations too high. I know its not what you were hopeing for but its a start. My feelings for you are real I hope you know; I just need to give things some time.

Love, Billy

It was no sonnet, but it would do the trick: dated just a week earlier, it was indisputable. I was sitting next to Anise on the couch and watching her carefully as she read it. She sat up straight and barely held the page. I had never been this close to her. Somehow she still had that regal air about her; no amount of betrayal could destroy it, it seemed.

"What's the cream for?" she asked. I guess she hadn't read it that carefully.

"His skin condition," I said.

"Oh." She replied. She hadn't a clue what I was talking about. She hadn't been the one lying next to Billy all these months. She looked at the letter some more. After a long while, she said, "But this is dated just a week ago."

There was a girl I once knew who was beautiful and kind, but naïve as dirt. That's what it takes to be a capital-H Heroine.

And though she was lovely and talented, men always crushed her and left. A mutual, male friend told me how he could see the thing in her that you could want to ruin. He called it the Desdemona Complex. Men desired her but couldn't stand her simple goodness, her trust. With her purity came the opportunity for a game—a chance for men to play out their own evils. Anise and I sat there some more and I listened to Billy's shameless lies pour out of her mouth: how we'd barely slept together, how I'd dragged him home from the bar when he was drunk and all but raped him. I was deciding between telling her the whole story or just enough so as not to hurt her too much, when suddenly Billy was rushing by us along the window outside the café. He stood there in the doorway with his hands out, looking vexed and confused. So it seemed Anise had a thing for arrangement as well. It occurred to me that maybe she had been watching out the window of Artifactual that afternoon. I got up and whispered something in her ear. "Okay," she nodded. I got my papers together and left. I had to nudge past Billy on the way out; he started to say something, but I was gone before he could finish.

A few weeks later, I heard that Anise had moved out of Billy's and into a boarding house downtown. I admired this, imagining her in one of those broken-down, wooden pioneer buildings full of old, widowed men. It went against type. Something in me relaxed. Despite the misunderstandings between us, I felt like a step had been taken that could make this story different from all the stories of the past. You see, I wanted the best for Anise, the same as I once did for Billy. Though we never agreed to it, in so many words, together we'd managed to expose a villain without getting a pillow over the face or a knife in the chest.

Over the next few months, Billy made life hard for me at the bar. Every day, he'd come in and sit at the wood until closing, staring at me, with what sense of injury I don't know. Once, he followed me home and it occurred to me he might try to kill me. But I reminded myself of what Billy was, and that this wasn't a real tragedy. I'd promised Anise I wouldn't talk to Billy anymore; and besides, the best thing I could do for him was not show him any generosity of feeling. Forgiveness. The only thing Billy understood about forgiveness was that it gave you an avenue for your next evil plan. Anise had told me about how she held Billy in her arms and listened to him crying about his mother, all the while she was going through treatment and Billy was in my bed whenever he had the chance.

Pretty soon I began hearing whispers amongst the regulars. Billy filling their ears with the wrongs he had endured. Now when I walked into the bar, they didn't smile up at me, they looked down into their pints. What was Billy saying? What must they think of me? It didn't matter. Anise was safe back out on the prairies and I could endure this. After all, despite what Billy told her, I had shown her how the trick was done, given her proof. Proof that was indisputable, not the kind that played on the mind like a flimsy dropped handkerchief, but the real thing, as banal as it was.

I thought this must be the end of it, surely. Then, one night, about six months later, Anise burst into The Hoof like the guest we'd all been waiting for, her hair in long crazy curls, eyes done up like a stage Egyptian, and her mouth a red varnish smile. She was thinner than ever, wearing a black dress that clung to her bones, and boots that put her over everyone's heads. Billy followed, with his hands shoved into his army pants. Apparently Anise had come straight from the plane to the bar. One of her supposed confidants told me that Billy and Anise had been performing love scenes all around the room. I hadn't seen this; in my years of serving, I'd learned how to turn certain customers into shadows at the edges of my good tables.

There were a few more incidents like this. Anise and Billy had come into The Hoof to celebrate Anise's thirty-fifth birthday. It seemed like a sober little occasion. But then followed the months when it was just Billy, night after night, staring at me from the end of the bar, more like the olden days. I got used to it. It became like the familiar dull ache in the shoulder that comes from holding the tray. You learn to ignore it and adjust to it at the same time.

So I was surprised, one day, to hear a passing comment from a regular that, despite Billy's loyal presence at my side every night, Anise and Billy were officially back together, that he was moving to the prairies to be with her. Who knows what he told her. It doesn't matter. It could have been anything, she would have gone back to him anyway. When I told Anise about

Billy and me, the first thing she said was that Billy had promised to marry her one day, in a castle on a hillside in Ireland. It had taken him two years to move two provinces, but she'd kept this castle in Ireland in her head. "Their love was," Anise wrote to me in an angry letter, "truer than ever." I will tell you now, I disliked her when I heard this. No change had come from the discovery I had forced upon them, from the proof I had offered up. No; in life, it turns out, proof means nothing.

There is another reading of Desdemona, I guess the one Anise found for herself: a love so sure of itself that it defies all the other stuff. Like their enduring love for each other was a magic that could confound and astonish everyone. Amongst some summer vacation photos I had seen, there was a picture of Anise and Billy at a Pitch 'n' Putt. Anise's standing in a silver headscarf against a miniature of Snow White's castle; she has a shit-eating grin on her face like she's made it to the Taj Mahal. In her deranged vision, Anise could make any dirt pile into Shangri-La. Could make a heaven of hell, twist the indisputable truth to shreds. Billy had made truth the enemy, a challenge to her love—a pure love, reignited by the frenzy of a duel. Billy had calculated correctly there.

All the while, I had stayed silent, not wasted my true self on this.

But what if I had insisted at all?

A few months after Billy and Anise had settled on the story that would allow them to continue, a girl named Lexi told me she had brought the whole thing up with Billy at Blue City. Lexi was a pretty girl, blue eyes and blonde hair like you wouldn't believe. But she worked at a rub and tug, and her breath always smelled bad. But she was good-hearted too, even though she dealt prescription drugs and was careless and always losing her little dog. She softened right up, or pretended to, anyway, when she told me how Billy had sighed, lowered his eyes, and told her how much he was still in love with me, and how I should have never talked to Anise. Things would have gone very differently, then.

Of course, I hadn't believed a word of it. It was one of the versions Billy kept on him, that he could whip up like a sketch artist on the street, doing portraits of passersby: you think you've left with an image of yourself, but really it's a stock figure with a few exaggerated and flattering touches. This was one Anise would never see, out of many she would never see, that Billy had sold to Lexi to give to me.

No, the way I saw it, being Desdemona means you get involved with a love so wicked, it demands you be as blind as a moron. As far as I could see, Anise's win was like that of an amusement park shooting gallery. It didn't matter the cheapness of the prize, you just kept giving up your coins 'til you got it. And from experience, Billy knew something I hadn't until now: to be a good con man, you need to take the story so far that people who love you are forced either to believe you or deem you a monster. Most people will choose what they can live with, and the con man knows this. Once someone's chosen the con, they can't go back. And meanwhile, Billy and Anise's mutual friends, who had momentarily taken sides, muttered moral judgments, but never seemed to see or say anything, were back to being Billy's friends. These same loyal friends still smiled and tipped me as I handed them their beer. Everybody readjusts accordingly.

It got me thinking again about that word "remorse" that Anise had used. Most people I'd met at the bar didn't have the luxury of remorse; they were too busy working and drinking. I remember Billy's friend Suzette used the same word about her art once: that it was a luxury she couldn't afford anymore. It occurred to me that maybe tragedy was best left to kings, or at least the upper business class and intelligentsia—those who have time to pace a castle floor or corner office in the sky, sit in front of their mirrors imagining the horror they have set into motion.

Tragedies were for the well-off. And betrayal and remorse only matter if they bring down a mighty and corrupt empire. Billy and Anise's kingdom didn't need that. Poverty's not a kingdom that changes hands; it just swallows what comes to it. So why was I so upset that I had failed? That nothing I'd revealed about Billy's character could save Anise, make her leave, change her course? This upset me far more than losing Billy had. Why? What did the poverty of their love have to offer? What had I missed? I was smarter. I spoke better. I was stronger. I came from a better place.

That's when I began reading George Orwell's *Down and Out in Paris and London*. Orwell came from good stock, but gave up respectability for a few years to live with The Poor in the infernal, underground hotel kitchens of 1920s Europe. I thought my answer might be here, that I might know why my story had gone the way it had: as though nothing had happened at all—no rise, no epiphany, and now no downfall.

From Orwell's observations, I could tell he had felt the envy I felt. It had led him to the epiphany, the answer to the question that had been bothering me all along. After living with The Poor, he concluded that the great redeeming feature of poverty is that it annihilates the future.

This was it. This was the key to Billy and Anise's world that I couldn't go down into. Somehow, Billy and Anise had escaped tragedy by staying in the middle of it. They could stand anything. For them, happiness was merely a series of moral lessons missed. Anise would forever continue her theatrics in front of the camera, and her eyes would shine with the excitement of love renewed, over and over again; and Billy, he would continue to operate and rot under the guise of union. In the ongoing present, there are no sins, only actions, and nobody dies from them. Well, if they do, it's only another action. Something for all those oil professionals, with their fifty-thousand-dollar trucks, to run over and obliterate.

Part V

In fact, the photograph tells us very little.

—**Susan Sontag**, *Regarding the Pain of Others*

That was how I finally settled things with Billy and Anise. As for me, I've gone about my business, published a few articles, finished my first term as a sessional at a college, teaching creative writing. Because of the recession, I guess, the college had to cut most of its weekend and evening arts courses, so they haven't asked me back. There are more artists than auto workers in this province now, but the only courses left for Masters of Literature are things like "Writing Through Yoga" and "Emotionally Expressive Writing." Like prison, the university has found the value of therapeutic writing.

Anyway, it means I'm back at the bar, for now. The friends I went to graduate school with have all moved away, managed to snag successful jobs in the academy despite the horror stories that there are none. The ones who have not quite finished yet come into my bar and look embarrassed when they see me. They sit in groups, and when I walk by with my tray, I try to catch what they're saying, to see if it's any different from what I remember. I serve them, I know, with the hostile smile of a waitress; and they tip me generously despite the fact that, for now, they make less money than I do. Once in a while, one of the successful ones returns to the city. When they come to The Hoof, we take a few moments to catch up on things. I can see in their faces that they think I am living in some way they don't quite understand, that perhaps I have escaped something they have not.

I have a new lover now. He tells me I am afraid to love. But mostly I think it's just that I don't want to be like everybody else. I tried to imagine what would happen to someone like Billy, who, now I can see, is like so many on the Avenue. Does he just go on forever like this? No disaster, just one meager pay period to the next. One crappy apartment after the next, half furnished. A new pair of boots every four years or so. Until he's lived out a lifetime more or less—then, one day, at around fifty or so, still working in a kitchen, some infection in the lung takes him. Perhaps there is a memorial at his last bar or restaurant and that is it.

I never saw Billy again, except once, the summer he returned here to finish some business. I caught a couple glimpses of him then, and he struck me as a portrait that doesn't change. "There he is, my Billy," I caught myself saying. Billy's beautiful face as white as wax under the streetlights at 1AM, violently ripping earphones out of his ears, turning into his last bar of the night. No doubt about to recite his life to some sympathetic waitress Anise will never know about. Billy dancing at Blue City with one of his many female friends, a stout girl with a dull look, who is in love with him. Like a magician, he raises her thick arm with his thin fiendish one and swirls her around with a grace that is out of place.

Occasionally, I entertain the idea that Billy did see something in me after all. Something he'd recognized in a flash. From time to time, the two of them irritate the edge of my thoughts, I don't know why; Billy, and that girl twirling for the camera: smiling over her shoulder, an exotic flower in her hair and a face shiny with tears—who never came back for the whole story. They turn in my head like some obscure hand. I don't know where they are now. I heard they've moved again, farther west, where they can't believe how temperate the weather is. The present life continues on somewhere else, I guess, against the telling of it. And I've stayed here, in this dull, infernal city—traded it all in, love, happiness and the rest, for the opportunity to tell you this.

NOTES

I would like to acknowledge the music, poetry, fiction and essays that were companion pieces to the writing of these stories. Some of their lines, insistent helpers, worked their way between my own.

• The epigraph introducing this collection is taken from Walter Benjamin's essay "On Some Motifs in Baudelaire" in *The Writer of Modern Life*: *Essays on Charles Baudelaire* (Michael W. Jennings, ed. The Belknap Press of Harvard UP, 2006).

"Fine Armour" includes:
• an epigraph taken from Virginia Woolf's essay "Street Haunting: A London Adventure" found in *Street Haunting*, The Pocket Penguins series (Penguin, 2005).
• the lines "I wonder were your heart is..." (etc.), from a poem cited in *The Women Troubadours* by Meg Bogin (Paddington Press, 1976).
• paraphrased lines from Stanley Kauffmann's essay "A Year With *Blow-Up*: Some Notes" (*Focus on Blow-Up*. Roy Huss, ed. Prentice-Hall Inc., 1971).

"The Cannibals" includes:
• an epigraph taken from "The Little Mermaid" by H.C. Andersen

(*Hans Christian Andersen: Fairy Tales*. Tiina Nunnally, trans.; Jackie Wullschlager, ed., Viking, 2004).

• paraphrased sections and quotations on the symbol of the bat, from *A Dictionary of Symbols* (Jean Chevalier and Alain Gheerbrant, eds., John Buchanan-Brown, trans., Blackwell Publishers, 1994).

• the lines "Your word is a gate..." (etc.), from "Psalm," a poem in *Prepositions for Remembrance Day* by Jon Furberg (Pulp Press, Vancouver, 1981). Commas have been added to indicate line breaks.

• a reworked line from *Madame Bovary* by Gustave Flaubert. The original is: "Emma was like any other mistress; and the charm of novelty, gradually slipping away like a garment, laid bare the eternal monotony of passion, whose forms and phrases are for ever the same." (A. Russell, trans., Penguin Popular Classics, 1995).

• lines spoken by Emma Bovary, Isabel Archer, and Anna Karenina which are the last direct-speech each character voices in *Madame Bovary*, *Portrait of a Lady* and *Anna Karenina*, respectively.

• a number of lines from "Summer Solstice" in *George Bowering: Selected Poems 1961-1992* by George Bowering (Roy Miki, ed., M&S, 1993), including one I rework: the original reads "Thea, never read my lines."

• the line "And where love ends, hate begins." from *Anna Karenina* by Leo Tolstoy (part 7, ch. 30), which can be found in any English translation.

• a line from *The Autobiography of J.M. Synge* that compares a bat's wing to a human hand that is part of a discussion on Darwin's theory of evolution. (Alan Frederick Price, ed., Dolmen Press, 1965).

"How To Read Your Lover's Favourite Russian Novel" includes:
• an epigraph taken from Robin Blaser's "Excerpts from *Astonishments*," transcribed tape recordings that are collected in *Even on Sunday* (Miriam Nichols, ed., National Poetry Foundation, 2002).
• direct quotations from Roland Barthes' *The Pleasure of the Text* (Richard Miller, trans., Hill and Wang, 1975), which act as self-help steps, and section headers, and sometimes appear in the body of the story.
• a reference to the first chapter, "Never Talk to Strangers," of *The Master and Margarita* by Mikhail Bulgakov, any edition.

"Jeanne's Monologue" includes:
• an epigraph taken from Charles Baudelaire's poem "The Little Old Women" in *Flowers of Evil* (Marthiel and Jackson Mathews, eds., George Dillon and Edna St. Vincent Millay, trans., New Directions, 1955).
• an epigraph taken from *The Arcades Project* by Walter Benjamin. I haven't been able to track down the source of the translation I have used; however, a different English version of

these lines can be found in [J66a,7] of Howard Eiland and Kevin McLaughlin's translation (Belknap, Harvard, 1999).

• Lines taken from the poem "Apparition" in *The Collected Poems of Irving Layton* (M&S, 1971).

• quoted and paraphrased lines (spoken by Thetis) from the section on Greek mythology, "The Origins of Humanity, The Deluge: Deucalion and Pyrrha" in *New Larousse Encyclopedia of Mythology* (Felix Guirand, et al., Richard Aldington and Delano Ames, trans., Robert Graves, intro., Prometheus Press, 1974).

• lines from Italo Calvino's *Invisible Cities*, Ch. 1. (William Weaver, trans., Harcourt Brace Jovanovich, 1972).

• the line "I have no life..." (etc.), which is a reworking of a line in the poem "To Constantina, Singing" by Percy Bysshe Shelley: "I have no life, Constantina, now, but thee."

• stage directions and Fellini lines which are paraphrased from Liv Ullmann's autobiography *Changing* (Albert A. Knopf, 1977). Liv Ullmann's lines are a direct quotation from the autobiography.

• a line from Robert Kroetsch's essay "The Moment of the Discovery of America Continues" in *The Lovely Treachery of Words: Essays Selected and New* (OUP, 1989).

• the line "You Must Marry the Terror," which is the last line in Kroetsch's poem "The Ledger" in *Completed Field Notes: The Long Poems of Robert Kroetsch* (M&S, 1989).

• Lines from Percy Bysshe Shelley's poem "Queen Mab."

• the line "Healing the wounds of these things..." (etc.) which is a quotation from Robin Blaser's *The Holy Forest*. *"Streams II*; Image-Nation 22 (in memoriam." (Coach House Press, 1993).

• a line from Elizabeth Smart's novel *By Grand Central Station I Sat Down and Wept* (UK General Books, 1991).

• a line adapted from M.M. Bakhtin's "Epic and Novel" in *The Dialogic Imagination: Four Essays* (Michael Holquist, ed., Caryl Emerson and Michael Holquist, trans., University of Texas Press, 1982).

• Jeanne's final line, which is from Phyllis Webb's poem "Non Linear," found in *The Vision Tree: Selected Poems* (Talonbooks, 1982).

"Love at Last Sight" includes:

• an epigraph taken from Charles Baudelaire's "Crowds" in *Paris Spleen* (Louise Varese, trans., New Directions, 1947).

"The Monster, or, The Deferred Subject" includes:

• an epigraph taken from the story "The Creature" by George Bowering in *The Rain Barrel* (Talonbooks, 1994).

• an epigraph taken from *Blonds on Bikes* by George Bowering, in a section called "Pictures," a collaboration between George and Angela Bowering, in a piece called "Prodigal" by Angela Bowering (Talonbooks, 1997).

• a line from the Duran Duran song "Girls on Film" from the album *Duran Duran* (EMI/Capitol, 1981).

• a line from the PJ Harvey song "Plants and Rags" from the album *Dry* (Too Pure, 1992).

"Where Were You In Canmore?" includes:
• the line "Music is the orphan's ordeal..." (etc.) taken from Nathaniel Mackey's *Discrepant Engagement: Dissonance, Cross-Culturality, and Experimental Writing;* "Sound and Sentiment, Sound and Symbol" (Cambridge UP, 1993).
• an epigraph taken from the song "Voices From the Wilderness" and lines from "World in a Wall." Both are from Martin Tielli's album *We Didn't Even Suspect That He Was The Poppy Salesman* (Six Shooter Records, 2001).
• a reference to the song "Take Me in Your Hand" by The Rheostatics, from the album *Introducing Happiness* (Sire Records, 1994).
• an excerpt from "The Descent" by William Carlos Williams, in *The Desert Music and Other Poems* (1954), collected in *Pictures From Brueghel and Other Poems* (New Directions, 1962).
• the line "You must learn to lose your heart..." (etc.) from Robert Duncan's poem "Structure of Rime XX" in *Roots and Branches* (New Directions, 1964).
• The line "Heard melodies..." (etc.) from "Ode on a Grecian Urn" by John Keats.
• the line "That detachement of the rose..." (etc.) from Sharon Thesen's poem "Day Dream" in *Artemis Hates Romance* (Coach House Press, 1980).

- the line "And how can..." (etc.) from William Butler Yeats' poem "Leda and the Swan."
- the line "He is so real..." (etc.) from Robert Duncan's "Imagining in Writing" in *Writing Writing 1942-53* (Trask House Books Inc., 1971).
- the line "Let sounds be sounds," which is from John Cage, *Themes and Variations* (1982), republished in *Compositions in Retrospect* (Exact Change, 1993).
- the lines "I went to the forest..." (etc.) from "The Lay of Skirnir" in *The Poetic Edda* (Carolyne Larrington trans., Oxford University Press, 1999).

"The Sitter" includes:
- an epigraph taken from John Berger's essay "Penelope"; the line "hope is a long affair" from John Berger's essay "Correspondence with Subcomandante Marcos: [...] III. How to Live with Stones"; and an excerpt from Berger's essay "Against the Great Defeat of the World": all in *The Shape of a Pocket* (Vintage International, 2001).
- an epigraph and other lines taken from H.D.'s poem "Eurydice" in *Collected Poems 1912-1944* (New Directions, 1983).
- paraphrased passages from *Portraiture* by Richard Brilliant (Reaktion Books, 1991).
- excerpted and paraphrased passages from Horst W. Janson's *Janson's History of Art: The Western Tradition* (7th edition, Penelope J. E. Davis, et al., eds., Prentice Hall, 2006).

• paraphrased (from memory) narration from the BBC documentary *How Art Made the World,* Episode 2: "The Day Pictures Were Born" (Dr. Nigel Spivey, host. Region 2, BBC, DVD, May 30, 2005).

• a full fragment from *Sappho: A New Translation by Mary Barnard* (University of California Press, 1958). I have added the notation (brackets and dots).

• a paraphrased section from Baudelaire's book *My Heart Laid Bare, and Other Prose Writings* (Ariana Reines, trans., Haskell House Publishers, 1975).

"To The Dogs" includes:

• an epigraph taken from Joy Division's song "Dead Souls" from the album *Still* (Factory, 1981).

• an epigraph that is a line spoken by Meryl Streep's character Helen Archer in the movie *Ironweed* (HBO et al., 1987), based on the novel *Ironweed* by William Kennedy.

• half a line from The Carpenters song "(They Long to Be) Close to You" from *Close to You* (A&M, 1970).

• an epigraph taken from Kristin Hersh's song "Gazebo Tree" from the album *Strange Angels* (4AD, 1998). I also name a bar in the story The Rainy Gazebo, after a line in the song.

• an epigraph from John Berger's essay "Ralph Fasanella and the Experience of the City" in *About Looking* (Pantheon Books, 1980).

• an epigraph from Susan Sontag's book *Regarding the Pain of*

Others (Picador, 2003).

• an epigraph and a paraphrased line on how poverty annihilates the future taken from chapter three of George Orwell's *Down and Out in Paris and London* (Penguin Books, 1989).

ACKNOWLEDGEMENTS

Earlier versions of some of these stories have appeared in *Dandelion, The Capilano Review, Matrix, Tessera, Arts Vancouver, Judy, Splurge,* and *The Dolphin Newsletter* (Aarhus University English Institute). Thank you to the editors. Special thanks to editors Anne Stone, Wayde Compton, and Ryan Knighton for their observations, advice, and company. Thank you to readers of these magazines, and to the audience members who approached me with their comments. In particular I would like to thank: Sharon Thesen, Michael O., Robin Blaser, David Farwell, Meredith Quartermain, Mark McCawley. Your supportive letters and words were encouraging during the long writing process. Thank you to friends who read various parts of the manuscript or discussed ideas with me: Jasmina Odor, Ben Lof, Hannah Calder, Theresa Cowan. A number of these stories began in Maureen Medved's Summer Prose Workshop at UBC, where I sat with a number of good, critical readers and writers. Lisa Roberton's class "Of Walking" at The Kootenay School of Writing introduced me to the concept of the Flâneur.

Thank you to my father, my second reader, for teaching me to reach this way and that, and for providing a world full of books, travel, play, music, poetry, and art throughout my childhood (on top of all the regular dad stuff). Thank you to my mother, my hero and teacher, for her life, love, stories, and for trying to teach me grammar, usage, editing, discipline, and gut-truths. I began this collection as I was losing her, and its overriding theme of love and memory concentrated by loss and change was driven by this time with her.

Thank you to Carol and Mike Matthews, Alison and Alex, for their protection and for and providing a place for me to write. To Lynn Spink. To Megan Morrison, Mike Grill, Holly Laing. To my friends who lived with me in the landscapes and times that inspired these stories, in particular: Peter Van Den Bergh—who introduced me to the writing of Solvej Balle, Marina Allemano— who taught me Andersen, my extended family, Kirsty Smith, Zofia Wodniecka, Janne Vedel Rasmussen, Magda Grohman, Jody Shenkarek, Gavin Dunn. Thank you to The Empress Ale House and The Black Dog for providing the stage. Thank you to Roman Kartushyn for his enthusiasm and passionate aspirations to share a practical and lyrical life with me.

I am honoured to be published by NeWest Press and in the company of its authors. I appreciate and respect NeWest's mandate of taking chances on new writers and unconventional writing. I am not a realist writer; all characters in this book are fictitious; any resemblance to real people is purely coincidental. Thank you to Matt Bowes and Paul Matwychuk for their hard work and for making this a pleasant, collaborative process.

Thanks to Greg Vickers for the layout and design and to Dwayne Martineau for the author image. I am especially grateful to my professional, intelligent, and sensitive editor Jenna Butler, and to Doug Barbour for his experience, and his attentiveness to the local and contemporary writing scene—and to both of them for encouraging me to submit. I am lucky to have poets and teachers as editors of my prose.

Thea Bowering has been published in *The Capilano Review*, *Matrix*, *Dandelion*, *The Vancouver Sun* and *Scandinavian Canadian Studies*. A native of Vancouver and former resident of Denmark, she now makes her home in Edmonton, Alberta. *Love at Last Sight* is her first book.

NUNATAK